Awakening Fate

CHELSEA BIDDISCOMBE

CHELSEA BIDDISCOMBE

Contents

Trigger Warnings

The following story contains the following:

- swearing

- violence

- mentions of graphic blood shed

- dementia

- mental health struggles

If any of these things are going to affect your personal wellbeing, this may not be the story for you.

Dedication

To my family:

Thank you for always supporting my dreams of being a writer (and Dad, sorry I never took up professional golfing.)

To my kids:

Never stop believing in yourself. During the moments of doubt, look to me. I'll be believing in you every step of the way.

Epigraph

Fairy tales are more than true: not because they tell us that dragons exist, but because they tell us that dragons can be beaten.

-Neil Gaiman

Prologue

On the day of Haven's birth there were only a few people that paused their lives to welcome her to the world.

Her mother was in labour for seventeen hours before Haven was born. She held her as if Haven was the most precious piece of handmade glass. Delicate and almost impossibly small, with pink cheeks and a soft brown tuft of hair matted down on top of her head. While looking down at the new baby in her arms Haven's mother sent a silent promise out to the universe. A promise to protect her forever, at any cost, from the evils of the world. A promise to make sure her daughter knew what it was to be loved and cherished. A promise to make sure her daughter knew that she was wanted, even on her bad days, even on her grumpy days. Haven's mother would always lead with love first when it came to Haven. That was her promise to the universe.

Haven's father gazed down at his wife tenderly holding his new baby girl, tears of joy in his eyes. To himself he vowed to protect Haven with everything he had in him. He promised she would know what it was to feel protected and supported. No dream was too big, no ambition was too much. His daughter would forever have his support. He took one more breath, sending that promise out into the universe, and then moved to sit beside his wife on her hospital bed, ready to celebrate their healthy new daughter.

Haven's grandmother was busy taking dozens of pictures, her heart filled with glee at the promise of a future for their family. Looking over at her new granddaughter and the doting parents sharing a private moment, Betty sent out her own silent promise to the universe. Betty would always be there to create a safe place for Haven to be herself. Betty would do anything in her power to make sure that Haven knew what it was to feel free to be her own person. In a world that was so quick to try and change anyone the least bit different, Betty would be the barricade protecting her granddaughter from as much heartache as she could, while showing Haven the strength within to withstand any fools that would try to change her.

Three promises pledged out of the purest form of love, all for a soul that was barely hours old. Three protectors and one innocent soul. Love, protection, and strength. All things that Haven would lean on during the toughest moments of her life.

Angels didn't sing out from the heavens the day that she was born. There was no clashing of thunder, no shaking of the earth, and no holy light shining upon the hospital as she was born. It was nothing but an ordinary birth, and yet, as fate would have it, Haven would turn out to be anything but ordinary.

CHAPTER ONE

Nova

Years after everything was over Nova would remember the beginning, the start of it all, with crystal clear accuracy. The thing about beginnings is that they don't always announce themselves as beginnings. Sometimes they appear as any average day, starting the way every other day for the past hundred started. As Nova crested into adulthood all she new was a quiet life.

Her childhood was nothing spectacular. No big traumas or life-changing incidents happened while she was growing up. Her parents were happily married and, while she was their only child, their house always felt full of life and laughter. Outside of her home Nova was known as the quiet one in school. She was a natural wallflower and people had a tendency to look right past her. Nova wasn't one to break the rules or question authority. If blending into a crowd was an art form Nova would have been a master at it.

Her dark auburn hair was the only physical feature to separate her from the crowd. She had a round face and a softly pointed nose. No one noticed her amber eyes, but the light freckles that brushed underneath her eyes made her look exceptionally young, even in her late teenage years. All of her facial features stayed mostly hidden, as it was her habit to keep her long hair hanging down in front of her face, an unconscious shield in front of her eyes to shelter her from the world.

Her clothing choices usually stayed in the neutral zone as far as colour went. Nova went for comfort and warmth over any type of fashion attempt. Oversized sweaters, baggier jeans that sometimes needed a belt to stay up, and a decent pair of sneakers was all she usually wore.

Most of Nova's peers only knew her as the student who always sat upfront, who dressed modestly, and who rarely, if ever, broke the rules in search of an adrenaline rush. Even the students who had been in the same classes as Nova for years had a tendency to assume that she was the new girl in school. This usually meant that her social calendar was always empty, never receiving invitations to the latest school dance or whatever sports game was coming up. Nova didn't mind; instead, she was excited to spend her time at the local libraries or at home with her parents, playing Scrabble and watching cheesy eighties movies. It was a simple life and that was perfect for her.

One of the downsides to such a quiet existence was that, despite the fact that Nova had dreams, her quiet voice meant that people stopped asking her what she wanted and treated her like a background object instead of a person of substance. Even though she tried to tell herself that it meant very little to her what people thought of her, there were still days that felt lonelier than they needed to.

Nova worked hard on her studies through her teenage years and was rewarded by getting into her top college choice. Her good grades helped her receive a variety of scholarships, lightening the financial load for her parents. The only downside for Nova was that it was a college in another city, which meant saying goodbye to her parents and venturing out into the world on her own. It was a big life change, but it was a change that Nova had been dreaming about her entire life. Education was important to her, but so was finding her own way in the world.

Nova appreciated the opportunity to grow, knowing that she had to break away from her parents to grow out of her childhood and into adulthood. She loved them fiercely, but it was time for her to grow her own wings and fly the nest, so to speak. If she stayed in town to attend college Nova would always settle back into familiar habits and become the wallflower once more.

Nova's parents helped pack her up and moved her four hours away into a dorm room just on the edge of campus. They set up everything for her, helped her find the dining hall, and gave her an emergency credit card. After some tears, Nova's parents said goodbye, and as they walked away, Nova knew in her gut she was ready to take on her new adventure.

The start of the new school season kept her busy, and as the first semester started flying by, Nova became accustomed to living dorm life. Communal showers, dining halls, class sizes easily three time what she was used to, all of it helped bring Nova out of her shell bit by bit. She was even making a few friends in class who didn't seem to mind her quiet demeanor.

It wasn't until halfway through the first semester that Nova even thought about going home for the weekend to visit her parents. They had been giving her space to settle in but tried calling weekly for a few minutes just to keep in touch.

Nova came across her first real hurdle since leaving home in the form of midterms. While classes had seemed to be going well, the stress and anxiety brought on by the weight that exams carried in college was starting to fray Nova's nerves. After a particularly difficult midterm that she thought she was well prepared for (at least until she was sitting in the exam room, staring at the test, knowing she was going to bomb it, and the corresponding meltdown she had once she got back to her room) Nova decided she could use a break from it all. It wasn't like her to drop the ball like that on a test, and the only reasoning she could come up with was that she hadn't given her all while studying. Before she was able to spin herself into a depression about it, Nova's mother suggested a weekend visiting home.

In all honesty it didn't take much before Nova caved to her mother's demands and packed to visit home after her last midterm exam. Nova spent the train ride home catching up on some much-needed sleep and scrolling social media.

The taxi ride from the train station to her childhood house seemed to take longer than the four-hour train ride itself, despite it only being at best a ten-minute drive. Nova texted her mother multiple times from the back of the cab, an excited energy started to circle in her gut. It didn't occur to her that the lack of response from her mother was odd.

Lost in memories, Nova's mouth watered for her mother's pancakes and blueberry syrup as her living room window came into view. She was vibrating with excitement, and when the cab arrived at her home Nova had to restrain herself from jumping out of the taxi before paying the driver and getting her luggage from the back. Once her suitcase was placed on the sidewalk beside her, and the driver started pulling away, Nova allowed herself one deep breath to take it all in.

Walking up the red brick sidewalk, Nova noticed her father's blue SUV still in the driveway. Nova had left earlier in the day than planned, making it midday when she arrived. Her father should have been at work still, but she shook it off as an impromptu move on her father's part to be home when she got to the house.

Nova walked up to the door, and without hesitation, she opened it and let herself in. Before closing the door, Nova took one last look at the neighborhood that she grew up in. It seemed almost too quiet for the time of day it was. Turning back and fully going through that doorway, Nova was unknowingly walking out of the quiet life that she had grown to love, and into a life she would come to resent and fear.

CHAPTER TWO

Nova

Stepping inside the house, Nova set her suitcase to the side quickly, expecting to be bombarded with hugs by her parents. The foyer appeared to be vacant, and after waiting a moment to see if she could hear anything, Nova called out to her mom.

"Mom? Are you here?" Her voice echoed off of the empty walls. Something wasn't sitting right in Nova's bones. The house seemed almost hauntingly quiet, and not in the comforting way that Nova had experienced in her entire childhood.

"Dad? Are you home? I saw your vehicle in the driveway! Where are you guys?" Nova opened the closet to put her jacket away; and toed her shoes off, straining to hear any kind of sound, something to let her know what direction she would find her parents in. There was still no answer, just silence. Her mouth turned down in a half frown as she furrowed her eyebrows. Something was definitely off. Something seriously didn't feel right.

The air started to feel almost thicker inside, and as she stood there, waiting for any kind of an answer, she noticed when she breathed in that the air had a strange scent to it. Almost as if someone had forgotten to take the garbage out and left all the doors closed on a warm summer's day. Neither of her parents liked a cluttered space, so the house usually was fairly clean. That smell, though, that awful putrid smell. The longer she stood there, the stronger the smell had started to become. Where was it coming from?

Walking from the front entry way, down the hall and into the kitchen, Nova tried not to let the eeriness coat her senses. A small ember of panic had started to grow in her chest and Nova tried to dislodge it by breathing slow and deep. As she breathed Nova felt the air become heavy as it started leaving a sick feeling in her lungs. One step after another, Nova made her way around the main floor. Looking for any signs of life, like a half-eaten sandwich or the television turned on, anything to signal that someone was around.

After walking in a complete circle and finding nothing to suggest that her parents were actually here, Nova went back to her jacket to grab her phone out of the front pocket. Dialing her mom's number and waiting for the phone to connect, Nova started making her way back towards the kitchen.

Once the call connected on her phone it only took a second for the ringer on her mom's phone to go off in the drawer right beside the fridge, scaring Nova halfway out of her skin. The tone was loud and shrill, just what her mother would have needed to hear the phone from anywhere in the house. Nova opened the drawer and picked up her mother's phone, canceling the call. The room was once again enveloped in silence.

Nova took a minute to look her mom's phone over, seeing all the messages she had sent to her mom left unopened and unread. By the look of things, her parents didn't know she was coming early. That would explain why there was no one there to greet her, but where would her mom be and why wouldn't she take her phone with her?

It also looked like her mother missed two phone calls from an unknown number. It wasn't like her mother to ignore her phone, no matter how busy she was. And leaving her phone at home while she went somewhere, that was something Nova would almost bet money on that her mother would never do. Noticing that the battery on her mom's phone was almost dead, Nova placed her own phone in the back pocket of her jeans, and she looked around for her parent's kitchen phone plug-in. When she finally saw the charger plugged into the wall by the stove, her guts rolled and the panic that she was trying so hard to squash started to flicker to life again. There, plugged into the charger, was her father's phone. Either both of her parents forgot their phones at home, which was more than highly unlikely, or something strange was happening here.

Nova went over to her dad's phone to see if she could find any answers. He also had a few missed calls, that spanned the last couple of days. Putting his phone back down Nova started her search for her parents once more.

"Mom? Dad?" Nova moved onto the second level, calling out again and again, hoping someone would answer her, but the only answer she got was her own voice echoing off the stairwell. Sometimes her mom would try to sleep off a migraine in the middle of the day, but what were the chances her father was doing the same thing?

When Nova got to the top of the steps, she noticed that the door to her old bedroom was the only door closed in the entire hallway. The bathroom door, the master bedroom door, and the door to the study were all open, as if they were inviting her in to learn their secrets.

Nova started with looking in the bathroom, and when she didn't find anything amiss in there she kept on down the hallway.

The master bedroom was next, as it was straight across from the bathroom. The bed in the master bedroom had been made for the day, and a small voice inside Nova's head suggested an even scarier option. Maybe the bed hadn't been slept in the night before. Everything else looked normal in the room, but the rock in her gut just kept getting bigger. Wild scenarios had started flooding their way into her head, depicting a variety of horrible things that could have happened. The longer it took for her to find someone, the longer the panic in the pit of her stomach grew.

The furnace automatically turned on, kicking up the air in the master bedroom, and the sour garbage smell from downstairs was making its presence known in the bedroom, except it was getting worse and more intense. Nova's stomach rolled, and it was an effort to keep the contents of that stomach where they should be.

Trying to breathe out of her mouth as much as she could helped, but not enough to keep her stomach from trying to heave. Nova clenched her jaw and gave her stomach a silent order. She would not let the anxiety and negative thoughts win. Someone would explain everything shortly after this, and she would feel like a fool for thinking so many awful things had happened.

Nova stepped back into the hallway, only one more opened door to investigate. Her dad's study appeared as every other room had. Nothing looked out of place, but that smell lingered in here, too. Nova knew where she had to go next. There was only one other room on this floor to check out. Dread sent chills down her spine, but her feet moved of their own volition as Nova turned to her old bedroom door. The door itself was a faded blue that once used to be as dark as the night sky. The silver knob stared at her, taunting her, daring her to open it. Nova stepped cautiously down the hall, her heartbeat slamming in her ears as her palms became slick with sweat.

It wasn't until she was about to turn the handle that bile crept up her throat and her heartbeat was going so strong and fast that it felt like it would break a hole in her chest. Instinct was screaming at her that something wasn't right.

Coming home was supposed to be like a dream, but this was the moment that Nova knew it had turned into a nightmare instead. The smell had gotten so bad, and it was refusing to dissipate from her sinuses. She could feel it burning the inside of her nose as her eyes started to water from the strong odor.

Nova reached out and, with a shaky hand, turned the door handle. Her feeble attempt at trying to push the door open failed as something heavy seemed to be in the way. The shock of not being able to easily open the door stumped Nova for a second, as she threw her whole body into it. It took a moment before she could feel whatever was blocking the door slide across the floor. After pushing a little harder, the door eventually gave way and Nova half-stumbled and half-fell into her old bedroom. The sight that greeted her did her the service of emptying her stomach of all its contents in one go on the floor right in front of her.

There was blood everywhere.

CHAPTER THREE

Haven

The sun was shining as the wind warmed her face, and there was a sweet smell in the air. Haven walked by the cherry blossom trees outside of the building, wishing she could sit and relax underneath them. It would be easy for her to lose a few hours on the bench there, daydreaming and reading.

Holding her bag close to her side, Haven pushed her long brown hair behind her ears and walked past the trees to the entrance of the building. The day had started out with typical early summer weather. Cool enough in the mornings to need a light sweater, but by the end of the day a simple t-shirt would be plenty. To go along with the dark denim jeans she was wearing, Haven chose a simple green V-neck t-shirt and paired it with a light black cardigan. Catching her reflection in the glass door to the building Haven took a second to admire the somewhat stylish outfit she managed to put together.

A moment later she was in the building and all thoughts of summer and warmth melted out of her. The waiting room she stepped into had cement walls and three rows of black metal chairs, all of which were empty at this time in the morning. Further into the room there was a check in desk with a nurse sitting behind it, working away at her computer. The clipboard sitting in front of the nurse for visitors sat empty, but Haven figured it was still early. Wishing the nurse a good morning, Haven filled out the appropriate boxes, stating her name and the patient that she was coming to see. After letting the nurse double check her ID and listening to the list of visitor rules, rules Haven had memorized by now, Haven just smiled and nodded.

"Just take a seat. Someone will come and get you when they're ready for you." Haven nodded her thanks and then sat down and waited until she was called in. She knew this waiting room well; she was in it at least once a week, often enough to know the names of most of the nurses and security guards. In fact, she had been going there for well over a year now. The grey walls were dull against the bright colours outside, and the metal chairs made the room feel cold and impersonal.

"Haven Conners? We're ready for you." A nurse appeared beside the security door and led Haven through it. There was very little small talk as Haven followed the nurse around every twist and corner. The doors to some of the rooms were propped open, showing some patients ready for the day. Other doors remained closed and behind one or two of them Haven could hear a nurse arguing about medication with someone. While the nurses usually had friendly smiles for Haven, it never distracted her from the fact that this was an institution, and not every patient here was here by choice.

Haven's footsteps echoed down the last hallway to her grandmother's room. The door opened as they approached as another familiar nurse came out, jotting down notes on her clipboard. The nurse leading Haven instructed her to enter, letting her know there would be someone at the nurse's desk just outside the room if she needed anything. Both nurses smiled at Haven and then went on with their jobs, leaving Haven standing just outside the room of her only living relative.

Betty, Haven's grandmother, had been a patient there for over a year now. Betty's mind had started to deteriorate at an alarming rate about two years ago. It was almost as if one week she was fine and the next week she had forgotten how to take care of herself. It became apparent that Betty couldn't be trusted to take care of her daily needs safely, as she couldn't even remember to turn the stove off or wear shoes outside in the winter. Being the only living relative, it fell to Haven to make the tough choices and she eventually decided a home would be the best place for Betty.

At first Haven tried putting her in a simple home with minimal supervision, but it turned out that Betty needed more medical attention than they could give her. A twenty-four-hour secure home where she would be able to come and go as she pleased would have worked well, except that lucid moments were becoming rare for Betty, to the point where she couldn't tell reality from fiction most days. It wasn't just a matter of forgetting where she was or getting lost on the way back to her room. Betty would have entire days where she believed she was from a different time and place. There were also days where Betty was sure that Haven was Hansel and she was Gretel, and that they had to set the witches' house on fire to get away. Mix that with an increasingly dangerous heart condition that needed constant monitoring and there was no way around it. Betty required full-time nursing care and a monitored environment.

Haven hated the fact that she couldn't take care of Betty herself. She had given it a try and it almost ended up in disaster. Thinking back on it Haven still couldn't get the memory of her grandma trying to light her mattress on fire out of her head. Haven had been in another room making dinner at the time and, according to Betty, she was fighting a spirit no one else could see. The smoke detectors went off and Haven ran into the room to see her grandmother trying to feed the flames with whatever she could grab. Luckily neither of them were hurt, but unluckily Haven knew at that moment she was in over her head. It was clear that Betty belonged somewhere with more help and supervision. The guilt of institutionalizing her own family ate away at Haven, but she had no other option.

Haven started visiting Betty in the institution every week and for the first bit Betty wouldn't even look her in the eye. Determined, Haven tried everything to reach her, but it wasn't until she brought an old book of fairy tales in that she got a reaction. The book itself was worn, the binding had frayed slightly and the words on the cover were starting to wear off. The edges of the pages were starting to yellow, but to Haven it was more precious than the rarest jewels. The book had been passed down in her family from generation to generation, mother's reading it to their children, grandmother's reading it to their grandchildren. Haven had so many warm memories centred around the book.

When she brought it in to read to Betty, Haven knew it was a long shot. Betty's heart was failing her, and her mind was slipping away, yet Haven was willing to try anything to reach Betty.

Only, it worked almost to well. After reading to her for a few hours Betty would then go around institution ranting about characters from the very fairy tales that were being read to her as if they were actual people. The doctors and nurses tried to gently suggest that it was all in Betty's head, but the more they would deny it the more Betty was sure that these characters existed. In Betty's mind Little Red Riding Hood and Peter Pan were alive, and to suggest otherwise would rile her up beyond the point of reason.

Eventually the nursing staff asked Haven to stop reading the stories to her grandma. Betty's doctors agreed that without Haven's weekly story time, these characters would fade from her memory and Betty would be an easier patient to handle.

However, it only took a few weeks before Betty took a turn for the worse, becoming fussy about her good days and downright impossible to deal with on her bad days. She would have tantrums and throw her food dishes against walls, and that was when she wasn't throwing insults at every nurse and orderly that came into her room. Instead of improving her condition, it just got worse. Her memory was almost obsolete and fading fast, and her vitals were worsening by the day.

After a few very stressful visits where her own grandmother couldn't even recognize her and wouldn't settle down long enough to visit without being sedated, Haven had reached her breaking point. She wasn't a doctor, but Haven knew in her gut that taking away the one thing Betty loved was no longer working. Betty didn't have a lot of time left and Haven didn't want her to spend it medicated and merely existing.

She met with the doctors and told them she was going to read the book to Betty again. The doctors agreed, albeit reluctantly, and over time it became clear that the only thing keeping Betty calm and giving her the rare lucid moments were the stories that Haven read to her. Within days of reading to her again, Betty started having more lucid days, and her tantrums were slowing to a minimum. The doctors weren't quite sure how it was happening, but it was almost as if part of her missing memory returned to her during those visits. She would talk to the nurses for hours after Haven left about raising her granddaughter on her own and the adventures that they used to share. The nurses enjoyed seeing the attention that Haven gave her and after every visit Betty would beam about the granddaughter that never forgot about her.

Haven was her only visitor, which didn't surprise anyone. Haven's parents only had one child, and then they both passed away while Haven was still young, leaving Haven in Betty's care. Over the years they became close, bonding over their shared loss. Instead of large Christmas feasts

Betty and Haven would order in a festive meal from the local diner and sit together to watch *It's a Wonderful Life*. While other teenagers were haggling money out of their parents' wallets for weekend shopping sprees at the mall, Haven would join Betty on the front porch for a cup of tea while they quietly read their respective books. It was a quiet upbringing full of mutual respect and support.

This visit was the same as every other and there was beauty in the simplicity of it. Every time Betty saw Haven coming she sat up straight, fluffing the pillows behind her for comfort, ready and eager to listen for the next few hours.

"Hi Grandma. How are you feeling today?" Haven put her coat and purse down and pulled the chair over to the bed and got herself comfortable. Haven usually tried to pull a few minutes of conversation out of Betty before jumping into reading. Some days it worked, and some days Betty's sole focus was that book and the characters within its pages.

"Sleeping Beauty. Today I want to hear about Sleeping Beauty." Wide eyed and ready to listen, Betty couldn't take her eyes off of the book. Her childlike innocence had shone through during these moments, which were beautiful and sad all at the same time. There wasn't much that Haven wouldn't do if her grandmother asked, immediately knowing where in the book the story was located, her fingers finding the way.

"Sleeping Beauty, you say? Hmmm. We haven't heard from her in a while." Before Haven could start, Betty suddenly put her hand on Haven's, causing Haven to look up from the book and into Betty's eyes. Wide eyed Betty, with a concerned look on her face, leaned into Haven. The sudden change in her composure was slightly alarming, as if someone flipped a switch in Betty's brain.

"She's in danger, grave danger. We need to help her, or she'll die." Betty said it so matter-of-factly and it took Haven by surprise for a moment.

She could hear her heart in her ears, stumped on what to say to that for a moment. Before Haven was able to pull herself together Betty let go, sat back up and waited for Haven to start the story. It was over so quickly that Haven wasn't convinced it had even happened. Taking a deep breath, Haven gathered her composure and continued looking for the story.

"Don't worry Grandma, no one is dying on our watch." Going along with it Haven played into the warning. Betty grinned and with that, Haven turned her attention to the book in her lap and started reading out loud about good versus evil in the fight to save a young girl's life. Betty hung on to every word Haven uttered. It didn't take her long to work her way through the story.

It took Haven two-and-a-half other fairytales on top of Sleeping Beauty before her voice needed a break. Promising Betty that she would be right back, Haven stood up to stretch and to go fill her water bottle in the hallway. The halls were still quiet, not much commotion happened around Betty's room. Haven took an extra moment to stretch and drink the cool water from her bottle. These visits were precious, and Haven knew that there would never be enough of them. Every time she visited and saw how far Betty had slipped Haven knew the inevitable was coming, and the ache in her heart grew stronger.

When Haven made her way back into the room, Betty was on the edge of the bed in tears, almost on the verge of hyperventilating. Haven rushed to her grandmother and put a hand on her shoulder as a gesture of comfort.

"Grandma, what's wrong? Are you ok?" Betty took a few shuddering deep breaths and turned her blood-shot eyes to her granddaughter. The concern from earlier was back and this time it was paired with fear.

"You stopped at the worst part. That left her suffering. We can't stop a story in a place that leaves the characters with no hope. You must always follow through the story. Give them hope and let them see that there will be an end to the suffering." Betty had grabbed on to Haven's arm for a moment before leaning back into her own bed. Haven sighed and fished a spare Kleenex out of her bag, handing it to her grandmother. Moments like this always left Haven wondering if she was still correct about not taking the stories away from Betty. Instead of responding to Betty's concerns, Haven picked the book up and continued on with the last story, only stopping when it was over.

As odd as it was, this wasn't the first time that Betty spouted strange advice about hope and fear and suffering in a story. Betty was always giving Haven strange advice and most of it sounded as if it should be coming out of the mouth of a child. It would be easy for Haven to brush it off as the crazy mutterings of someone who was so lost in their own minds that reality just didn't appeal to them. However, this woman had raised her, had taught her how to be a good human, and the least she could do was listen when Betty talked, hold her hand when she was scared, and show her that someone loved her, that someone was there for her.

After the visit was over Haven headed straight home, willing the headache that was forming to hold on. As special as it was to have those visits with her grandma, it was also exhausting and took an emotion toll to see the woman who helped raise her deteriorating in front of her. Haven walked into her apartment and set her things on the counter. Taking a long look at the storybook, Haven could appreciate it for the history that it held. Such a strange item for her grandmother to be obsessed with. No matter what the situation, if the book was there, Betty wouldn't take her eyes off of it, like it held some mystical thrall or beacon, but to Haven it just looked like a book. Tossing it on her bed, Haven went about her nightly ritual, getting to bed at a decent hour and falling asleep straight away.

Silver eyes. Dangerous silver eyes, staring her down. With a jolt of fear, Haven opened her eyes to find herself in an alarming situation. She had gone to bed in her one-bedroom apartment and somehow woke up in a dark forest. Still wearing her pajamas, her breath coming out hard and fast, she looked around, trying to find clues as to where she was and how she came to be there. The last thing she remembered was being in her home, did someone take her from there? Drug her to mess with her memory?

Her heavy breathing was starting to make her lightheaded. Looking down Haven noticed the cool dark dirt contrasting against her pale, cold bare feet. Where were her shoes, or her even jacket? She started rubbing her hands up and down her arms, trying to warm them up but also comfort herself. Her brain was in a fog and the longer it took to figure out what was going on the more Haven's panic grew.

Suddenly, in the distance, she could hear someone crying. Not just a whimper, but someone was full on sobbing. Without fully understanding why she did it, Haven started walking towards the noise. Perhaps if someone else was stuck out there they could help each other out. Her steps were a little shaky to start off with and Haven couldn't stop her eyes from darting all around, looking for any kind of clue, or danger, to help the brain fog lift.

As she got closer to the noise, Haven saw what looked like a poor young woman being cornered by a large, snarling wolf. The woman tried to dodge left and dodge right, attempting to get around the feral beast, but no matter which way she ran, the wolf was right there, playing with her, feasting on her fears. Where did this woman come from? There were no vehicles or roads around, how did they get out here, wherever here was? None of this made sense.

Haven was at least fifty feet back in the shadows, making her invisible to the woman. The wolf appeared to be getting restless, snapping its jaw at the woman, and Haven knew in her gut that this wasn't a story that would have a happy ending.

The snarl of the wolf vibrated down her spine, sending chills up and down her arms. For a split-second Haven was glad that the wolf wasn't focused on her. Instead, it was dead set on this poor woman, who looked like she had been through quite the struggle already. Her clothes were muddy and torn, the palms of her hands were crusted with dirt, and her hair appeared wild and knotted. From where she stood in the shadows Haven could see the tracks of tears falling down the woman's face and the sound of the sobbing was becoming more erratic.

Unable to just keep standing by, watching from the shadows, Haven made the decision to find a way to help, maybe distract the wolf for just a moment, to give the woman a chance to get away.

The woman glanced into the shadows and, without realizing it, made eye contact with Haven. It was in that moment, that brief connection, that felt like a kick in the gut. The moment Haven decided to lift a leg to take a step forward, the wolf snapped its head around, turning those silver eyes on her. Haven's foot hovered in the air for a moment before she placed it forward as if she was coming closer, but the wolf snapped its jaw at her hard enough that spit flew out of its mouth. It was enough to make Haven back up a few steps. There was no way this was actually happening, this had to be a dream! A dream, this was a dream. Haven kept repeating it to herself, wishing for it to be true. If it wasn't, did she really want to take on a wild, rabid wolf by herself? Could she even do anything without any weapons or anything to defend herself?

Satisfied that it had scared her enough to back up, the wolf then returned its attention towards the young woman, who was trying to run away while his attention was fixed upon someone else. He was on the woman's back within seconds, his jaw clamped around her neck. The woman screamed as she fell to the ground, blood pouring down her neck and an inhumane snarl came out of the wolf's throat as he shook the woman by the neck once, and then twice.

Haven hadn't seen anything quite so gruesome in all her life, the contents of her stomach threatened to evacuate as she willed it down by holding a hand in front of her mouth. Once the woman was dead, the wolf lifted its head up and looked at her. Blood dripped down its jaw and those silver eyes dared her to do anything about it. Haven went to take a few more steps back involuntarily, and the wolf pounced, barring his bloody teeth her way, but never made it to her before she woke up.

Haven opened her eyes and started wildly thrashing her limbs around, trying to fight off the wolf. It took a few seconds before it registered to her that she was fighting with bed sheets and not a wild animal. Her breathing was out of control and her head started spinning as reality sunk in. It was a dream, she wasn't out in the forest, and there was no giant wolf trying to eat her. In an attempt to calm herself down Haven closed her eyes and took a couple of deep breaths. The sheets beneath her felt damp and her skin was slick with sweat. Her throat felt raw, and her mouth felt dry. Her stomach was turning, and she could feel bile creeping up her throat.

It all had felt so real. Seeing that woman being torn to shreds by that beast, it was the thing nightmares were made of. But what unnerved her the most was the memory of those silver wolf's eyes staring her down at the end, silently promising to come for her next.

CHAPTER FOUR

Nova

Blood. On the walls, on the floor, all over the bed. The smell kept washing over her as Nova gagged and retched while trying to remain standing, using the door as a crutch. The stench of decay, like meat left out for days, permeated the walls, floor, and bed. Looking down Nova confirmed that the lump holding the door closed, the one that she had to push out of the way, was none other than the brutally wounded body of her mother.

A scream built up inside of her raw throat but refused to exit her mouth. Her throat burned from the vomiting and the straining effort of trying to make a sound. It looked like her mother's body went ten rounds with a machete, deep cuts every which way. Blood soaked into her clothes, dying them a deep red. All color had seeped out of her face and her eyes, still open in a look of horror, were lifeless. It may have been the body of her mother, but her spirit was long gone, with no way to know how long she had been there like that. Sobs kept creeping out of Nova's throat, sounding anything but human.

For a moment Nova couldn't force herself to look anywhere else but at the corpse that laid in front of her. In the back of her mind, though, she knew there was something else in the room that required her attention. Out of the corner of her eye, she could make out another lump surrounded by more dark red stains. Turning her head slowly, hoping against all odds that her instincts of what it was were wrong, Nova saw yet one more sight that had her stomach heaving uncontrollably. Her eyes were burning with tears that she didn't even know she was producing. They slid down her face and pooled on her chin.

Over on the bed, in the same horrific cut up condition, was her father, only he seemed to have more damage, mostly to his throat. It looked like a wild animal had ripped it out. His body and his clothes had deep cuts all over and his face was just as lifeless. The scream stuck in her throat broke free.

Above him, written on the wall in what could only be blood, was a message. One word, enough to send a chill up her spine. Nova. Was it a message meant for her parents, a threat on the life of their child, or was it meant for her, written in their blood?

Chills ran up and down her spine, her stomach was in knots, and the world was spinning. Nova managed to stumble out of the room before she collapsed onto the hallway carpet. Her breath was coming in shallow gulps, shaking she tried to pull her phone out to call an ambulance, knowing her parents were dead but not quite understanding the weight of the situation.

Her fingers seemed to have forgotten how to work and she dropped her phone a few times before she could get three simple numbers dialed in. It took everything out of her to make that call, on the brink of a full-blown panic attack and psychotic break.

"911, what's your emergency?" The voice on the other end may as well have been a thousand miles away, the way the blood pumping in her head dulled any noises around her.

"My... my parents ... are ... blood. Send help. Hurt." Nova couldn't speak any louder than a whisper.

"Ma'am, can you repeat that again for me? Your parents are hurt? What injuries did they sustain?" Nova's hands and feet started to tingle with cold as she started shaking.

"I ... I don't ... um ... more hurt. Dead, I think ... just please come." From where she collapsed, she could still see her mother's lifeless, massacred body. She tried closing her eyes, but the images of her parents were burned to the inside of her eyelids, and her stomach kept rolling.

"Ma'am? Ma'am, stay with me, please. Did you say dead? What happened? I will send help, but I need to know where you are, and I need to know what the situation is. Is that something you can help me understand?" the voice on the other end asked urgently.

"Yes." Using her arms, Nova pulled herself around the corner, into the office, and propped herself up against the wall.

"Okay. Ma'am, are you yourself hurt?" She could no longer see them, but that smell was something she wouldn't be able to escape. She tried holding her breath to keep away from the smell, but it only made her more than dizzy.

"No ... no I'm ... not injured. Just them. Blood, an attack." The operator on the other line got her address off of her and promised help was on its way.

Time was moving far too slowly for her. The ambulance and the cops, they should have been there by now, and yet it felt like hours had gone by. Staring at the clock on the desk, watching the second-hand tick by, she couldn't understand why this was happening.

Who would do something like this? Her parents were not the type to be caught up in trouble. They were so dependable and ordinary it bordered on dull, and she loved them for that. They didn't even like road rage or gossiping about the neighbours. Nothing was making sense.

Her mind registered very little after that. Not the cops showing up, questioning her, or the coroner coming for the bodies. She paid little attention to the cops escorting her to their cruiser or to the drive to the police precinct.

When she arrived at the precinct, Nova was put in an interrogation room with a bottle of water and a box of Kleenex. The lead officer on the case started asking her question after question, asking her if the visit was planned, if her parents knew she was coming, and asking for the bus ticket to prove that she didn't get into town until that morning. The line of questioning would have offended Nova if she had been in her right mind. As it was, she didn't notice that the police were trying to rule her out as a suspect. After a few hours, it was obvious to the officer that he would not get anything else out of her. It didn't look like she was the guilty party, and her name written on the wall in blood seemed to imply that, had she come home a few days earlier, she wouldn't be sitting across the table breathing in air.

If she was a target, she would need police protection, at least until they knew for sure what was going on and if she was in danger. They could keep her at the precinct overnight, but the poor girl looked like a truck had run her over. Her eyes were bloodshot, and her response time was becoming slower and slower. The forensic team tested the blood on the wall while she was being interrogated, and it took almost no time at all to verify that it was, in fact, human blood.

With the hour getting late and nothing else to go on, no other leads, at least until the autopsies were done, they convinced Nova to let them hide her away in a motel on the other side of town, with a twenty-four-hour protection detail. It wasn't a permanent solution, but for the night, it was somewhere safe for her to sleep.

The officer that escorted her there did a sweep of the room, and explained to her that if anything happened, even something small, she was to run out of the room and make as much noise as she could. He even offered to have a female officer sit in the room with her, but Nova declined. Other than that, his only advice was to get some rest. The door clicked shut as he left, and Nova let the silence wash over her.

Nova had no one she could call. The only genuine family in her life had been her parents. Both of them were only children, and any long-lost relatives she may have had lived somewhere in eastern Europe and could barely speak English. Growing up, Nova didn't have large family Christmases or summers filled with rowdy family reunions. It never occurred to Nova that one day she would wish for a large family to fall back on.

Never feeling more alone Nova sat in the middle of the motel bed, her long, dark red hair damp from the shower where she scrubbed her skin raw trying, but failing, to feel clean, holding her legs to her, and rocking back and forth. Her cell phone sat on the bed in front of her, screen black, as if to taunt her for not having anyone to call. She had made no real friends at school yet, and none of the neighbours ever took an interest in her growing up.

Every noise made her jump, every shadow made by cars that drove by spooked her. She stayed far away from the door and windows. The complimentary TV stayed off and the iPod she kept in her purse was forgotten about. All that she had was the hum of the heater and the squeak of the bed as she rocked back and forth, comforting herself.

A cold burger sat on the table by the door, with equally cold fries, untouched. The officer that drove her to the motel insisted she eat something.

He said it would help ease her stomach. But every time Nova attempted to put anything near her mouth, that smell from her room reappeared, turning her stomach, and she had to spit it out or risk getting sick again.

Tears had left permanent streaks down her freckled face, her amber eyes blotchy and swollen, and yet a fresh set would surface every so often. Dehydration was the least of her worries, but all the crying had left her with one hell of a headache.

While Nova knew the police wouldn't admit it to her, they were obviously baffled after taking in the scene at her parent's house. It didn't appear as if anyone had forced their way into the house. She knew as well as they did that the only room that looked like it had a struggle in it was Nova's old bedroom. It was almost as if someone had lured her parents into that room, only to murder them. How that person, or persons, got into her old room in the first place was still a mystery. Nova hadn't received any type of threats while away at school, so the only piece of evidence suggesting that there was a threat to her life was her name left on the wall in blood.

Nova kept rocking, keeping the image of her dead mother front and centre in her brain. Another wave of tears washed over her face as she realized she would never again get to hear her mother's voice. Never again would she hear her mother laugh, and never again would she be able to hug her mom. She wouldn't be able to make breakfast with her dad. His dorky jokes were gone, and there would be no more helping him around in his workshop. Her parents were gone. Nova hadn't been out of high school for long. She had the rest of her life ahead of her, and her parents wouldn't get to see another second of it. It was official. Nova was alone in life.

Sleep eluded her as Nova tossed and turned most of the night, counting the hours on the clock until sun rise. Every light in the motel room remained on, Nova's attempt at keeping the demons at bay. If someone was going to sneak up on her, she wanted it to be very obvious to the cops outside. She would get up off of the bed every hour just to check that the cop car was still parked in the same spot, and that there was an officer still inside of it. The last thing she needed was for this to be some type of sketchy horror movie, where the cop outside disappeared just long enough for the murderer to get his victim. Maybe she had watched too many movies, but she'd be damned if she fell prey to a murder in some cheesy way.

By the time morning came, there were so many questions on a continuous loop in her head. Was she in danger? If the suspect left her name in blood, she had to assume someone had been looking for her. If she had been home already would her parents still be alive, would the killer have left them alone? If she hadn't planned on coming home, would her parent's dead bodies still be lying there, without a soul in the world knowing what had happened? It all boiled down to one question. Was it her fault her parents were murdered? This type of thinking was driving her mad, but she couldn't shake these thoughts. A knock on the door pulled her out of her own mind. An officer was there to escort her back to the precinct, where she would hopefully be given an update stating that they caught whomever they were looking for and she was free to go.

Unfortunately, that wasn't the update she was given. Instead, it was explained to her that, with almost zero leads, they weren't comfortable allowing Nova out of their sight. It was explained to Nova that they wanted to keep her in custody indefinitely. Nova wanted to argue with them, tell them she had a life to get back to, and funerals to plan. She wouldn't be able to properly mourn the loss of her parents if she was spending her days being questioned about the horrific events. The officer she was talking to, however, was insistent that the threat to her life was still severe enough to warrant the full force keeping her safe. Nova knew the officer was right, but deep down she just wanted to be left alone. That night she was brought back to the motel room, provided a meal that she didn't feel like eating, and then left alone again with the thoughts and nightmares swarming around in her brain.

The next few days went by the same and Nova found herself slipping further from reality. The days began to blur together as a routine had formed. She would be questioned by detectives and cops during the day, asking her the same questions over and over, telling her that despite their best efforts, no new information had made itself known. The forensics team was having issues finding any evidence of anyone being in that home that shouldn't have been. No foreign fingerprints, no shoe prints outside or inside, nothing to suggest anyone had broken in. Even in Nova's room, there was nothing out of the ordinary. The police swabbed the room from top to bottom, with nothing presenting itself as a clue.

The bodies themselves didn't even hold any clues. Every wound was from a sharp blade, but the coroner couldn't tell what kind of blade it was. All he could tell the police was that it looked like the work of a professional. The cuts weren't sloppy or rushed. Whoever attacked the couple knew what they were doing, and they took their time doing it. This wasn't some crime of passion. Someone calculated the attack. It was as if someone wanted to punish her parents for something, get revenge.

At night, Nova would lie on the hotel bed and stare at the ceiling until exhaustion took hold. She couldn't fall asleep and so she would close her eyes and wait, sometimes for hours, before her mind slipped away for a few hours of rest. It was the third night in the hotel that changed everything. That was when the dreams started.

It would start out in a dark, concrete room. The air was heavy with a chill and dread hung around like a foul stench. The concrete floor was more of an illusion than anything else. When she stepped forward, her foot sank, and in an instant she was calf-deep in wet cement. It was thick and stuck to her bare feet whenever she tried to pull her leg up. Nova tried to move her feet to the rickety wooden staircase along the opposite side of the room, the only way out that she could see. Her movements were slow since she couldn't move her feet very fast, and she was out of breath before she was halfway across the room. Trying not to panic, she focused on lifting one foot up at a time and placing it in front of her. Breathing in, lifting her leg, placing her foot down, and then breathing out, she made it to the other side.

Once she reached the bottom of the stairs, all the hair on her arms stood up straight, as if her body knew that she wasn't alone in the room. If she listened closely, she could hear it. There was a growl in the dark, in the shadows. Once she noticed its presence, the growling got louder. Nova put her hand on the rail and one foot on the bottom stair but hesitated going any further. She didn't know what was on the other side of the door. She couldn't stay where she was, not while there was something lurking in the shadows. Making up her mind, she attempted to sprint up the stairs, only the wooden stairs turn into pits of tar, each step burning her where her concrete covered skin contacted the wet tar. She only made it up three stairs before the staircase disappeared and she fell to the ground. Her feet and the bottoms of her legs felt as if they were on fire. The concrete was drying, and the tar stuck to any skin the concrete hadn't touched.

Pulling herself up to stand, Nova noticed the staircase had turned into a large oak tree, and the basement had turned into a forest. Tall, dark trees stood all around her. The air was thick and humid, her surroundings were eerily quiet. The only exception to that being the growling. It started getting louder, and it sounded like it was coming from right behind her. Nova turned around, putting one of the large trees at her back, and daring to look at what she feared. When she saw what the noise was coming from, a scream bubbled up in her throat and echoed throughout the forest.

There was a large snarling amber wolf with silver eyes watching her every move, his hackles up, ready to attack at any minute. Nova couldn't move, as her body was paralyzed with fear. From where she stood, she could see drool dribbling from between his sharp teeth. Time slowed down and Nova could feel each heartbeat as if in slow motion.

For a brief moment Nova was rescued from the daring gaze of the wolf as he turned his head to look behind him and snapped at something in the dark before returning his attention to her. Nova knew she couldn't just stand there forever. Soon the wolf would lunge, and she would be toast.

She tried darting to the left as best as she could with her cement covered feet, but the wolf countered that by darting to his right and putting his body in-between her and her way out. She tried going right and as if he knew that's what she was thinking, he would go left a split second before her. After trying this a few times, Nova could feel any hope of getting out alive drain from her body. Her only option was to turn and run, creating the perfect chase scenario for the predator. Nova made it two steps before the wolf was on her, lodging its jaw around the back of her neck and squeezing. Nova let out an ear-piercing scream and fell to the ground, with the wolf still attached to her neck in excruciating pain. The saliva from his mouth dripped down into her hair and down the back of her neck. She could feel his teeth sinking deeper and deeper into her flesh while the weight of his body kept her pinned to the ground. Before blacking out, she thought of her parents and the possibility of reuniting with them in the afterlife.

CHAPTER FIVE

Nova

Nova woke up with sweat on her forehead, out of breath, her pulse racing. The sheets around her felt damp as she clutched them in her hands, and there were tear tracks down her face. Her throat felt raw from the constant screaming throughout the night. It had become normal for her to wake up like this; the terrors in her mind rarely gave her any real rest.

Nova lay there, her harsh breathing the only sound in the hotel room, unable to move even an inch. She was paralyzed with fear, fear of what happened and the fear of not knowing how to feel safe. She stayed that way, knowing that the sun would come up soon and erase the shadows of her nightmares for a few hours at least. Until sunrise, she stared at the ceiling of the hotel room, counting her breaths as the terrifying images of her parents replayed over and over behind her sad eyes.

Why was it that the sun always promised a sense of security? The monsters under the bed were never as scary during the day. Life never seemed quite as hopeful as when the sun's rays danced through the window. Without it, there seemed to be no hope, no promise of a new day.

When the sun finally came up a few hours later, Nova felt the muscles in her body start to unlock and she felt safe enough to start moving around. Soreness from locked muscles plagued her from head to toe. Her head was pounding from lack of sleep and nutrition. Her appetite never came back, and she was feeling the consequences of her empty stomach. As Nova looked out the window at the sunrise, she mentally started a countdown of how many hours she had left before the darkness took over, before she could no longer fight the fatigue, before she would give in to the nightmares once again. It was a cycle that she had been stuck in since the very first night. A nightmarish Groundhogs Day with no end in sight, and no help in sight, either.

After waking up from the same nightmare for a fifth night in a row, Nova decided she couldn't just sit still anymore. Feeling like an animal in a cage, nothing was in her control. Nova couldn't shake the feeling that the darkness was getting closer and closer each night. She had tried talking to the officer the night before, asking if she could talk to a doctor about sleeping pills or anything that she could use to knock herself out. She was told that they needed her alert and clear minded in case there was a break in the case. Nova was losing her mind and the people that were sworn to protect were effectively locking her up, keeping her defenseless for whomever was chasing her. They were turning her into easy prey, and Nova was panicking.

There was something else at work here. Growing up, despite all the stories she was told, Nova always held the belief that monsters, while useful to teach a lesson in a book, weren't actually real. Her parents never came out and stated it directly, but using common sense Nova knew that stories were just that, stories. If someone were to ask her now, she would have a different answer. Whomever, or whatever, attacked her parents had to be a monster, or at least had to be someone with evil in their heart. No regular human would be able to do that to another human.

Nova knew deep in her soul that whatever was hunting her was evil in one way or another. With the echoes of her nightmares still ringing in her ears she felt that it wasn't an evil that the regular world would understand. There was more to it than that. She woke from her nightmares feeling the rage and spite vibrating off of the wolf. Her dreams were full of someone wanting to tear her to shreds, and her reality was that someone had already done it to her parents. Evil needed no reason to hurt others, and in her gut she knew it had turned its wicked eyes on her. It dawned on her that, while she was sitting in a motel room waiting for the cops to find evidence, she was wasting time. The longer they took, the closer the danger was getting.

From the outside, it looked like Nova was spiraling out of control. Suffering a loss like hers was an experience that would send any regular person into deep grief, but Nova was going through something even more. That she felt trapped and terrified meant that she hadn't even started processing her grief. The grief that she was trying to push down was causing her anxiety and paranoia to rise to dangerous levels. By the end of the fifth night, everyone and everything seemed to have a motive to want her dead. Who could she trust at this point when it seemed like no one was willing to come forward to help her?

On the sixth night, something in Nova snapped. She felt like a caged animal pacing back and forth with nowhere to go and no hope of escaping from her predicament. If she didn't do something, she would be dead by the end of the night. Nova felt that with every fiber of her being. Each night, when the hotel door closed with her inside, it felt like a predator was watching her.

But what could she do? Where would she go? She had no family she could go stay with, no friends across the country that would make her feel safe. She asked the cops when the next step would come, when they would find whoever did this so she could bury her parents and get out of town. Every time she asked, they gave the same vague answer. They were working on it and with no new leads; it was hard to say how long this would last. Nova finally stopped asking.

Instead, she spent her time plotting and planning on a way to escape, which to a reasonable person would have sounded crazy. No one ran away from the police, but Nova was no longer a reasonable person. Nova packed up her few belongings, including any leftover food, then waited for the officer's last check of the night. She ended up waiting until the middle of the night, when the officer on duty was fighting to stay awake in the car outside. Nova watched carefully through the blinds as the officer's eyes became heavier. The neighborhood they were in was quiet, there wasn't much traffic, and the lack of excitement ended up being the last piece of the puzzle. The officer couldn't stay awake and the moment the officer nodded off; Nova was ready.

She dragged the door open and, looking around the room one last time, told herself she was making the right decision. All she saw looking at that room was a trap, a cage, and somewhere she really didn't want to be the last thing she saw before she was murdered. Nova knew she was making the best decision she could in a terrible situation, so she slipped out the door, quietly letting it close, tiptoeing to the back fire escape as her sneakers started squeaking on the metal.

Holding her breath as she made her way down the fire escape to the ground floor, Nova did everything she could to be a silent shadow in the night. Once on the ground, she backed away slowly until she reached the back of the building. Once there, she took a glance back and noticed that the officer in the car hadn't moved an eyelash. No one had noticed a thing, no one was chasing after her, there was not one person on the planet that knew where she was or where she was going.

That made her more confident about her decision to run. If she could sneak out that easily, then what was stopping her parent's murderer from sneaking in right in the front of the cops? One last glance back and Nova took off down the alley, running in fear of what was coming for her, running in fear for her life, running for her own sanity, running from those silver eyes.

CHAPTER SIX

James

Leaning back in his seat, letting the cool draft from the airplane vents hit him in the face, James finally relaxed. The ice in the glass of bourbon clinked against the side of the cup as he placed it down on the side table. This had been a somewhat successful business trip for him, but not as successful as he would have liked. There was still one piece of the puzzle that he hadn't been able to put into place. It bothered him, the way an itchy tag on a fresh shirt would bother an average person, but it was something he planned on fixing soon.

But first, James had to head back to the office to give the board his latest update and to talk to his team. He had a new task for them, and it was something that couldn't wait another day.

James put up his long, blonde hair in a bun and stretched his knuckles. He noticed dried blood on his wrist and used his thumb to rub it off while checking his sleeves to make sure he didn't get any stains on his newest Armani suit. It wouldn't look good if he updated the board with evidence of his dirty work on his jacket, reminding them of exactly what he was out to do. It was up to him to do what needed to be done without reminding the board of how he achieved the goals they set for him.

They would already be in a somewhat unhappy mood when he let them know he wasn't one hundred per cent successful in his recent project. It was important that they knew, though, that while he didn't get the entire package, he didn't exactly walk away with nothing. And a little negotiation was to be expected in these kinds of deals. Nothing was ever really written in stone, and he could always nab the last bit in a later business arrangement, which is exactly what he had planned to do.

James had worked in the same company since he was a young man. It was a company that his family had built from scratch decades ago. From the ground up, they started out as a small marketing firm, and now they were one of the top four giants of the industry in the United States, and in various other countries. When he was younger, his father started him at the bottom as a gopher to teach him a lesson. No son of his was going to be handed a top position in any company just because of his last name. Instead, James would have to earn it by working his way up. Within six months, James had impressed a fair number of influential people, and not just because of his last name. He picked things up easily; he took initiative, and his ideas for helping the company grow were fresh and innovative.

Within two years, James had worked his way from being a gopher into having a corner office. He walked around with an air of confidence that some would find cocky, but it had helped him strong arm clients into doing what he wanted. Of course, he always backed his reputation up by hitting every goal he set out to achieve. He was known for being ruthless in negotiations, and yet it never seemed like enough for his dad. Not to say that he lived and breathed for acceptance that only a loving father could give him, but it was always a competition between the two of them. Two alpha dogs doing the dominance dance every time they were in the same room together.

Growing up, he and his father never saw eye to eye, so why should they start now? His father could approve or not, sooner or later he would be forced to retire, and James could take over the company entirely, a company that would flourish even more under his guidance. The board wouldn't stand in his way, and if they did, he would do what exactly what they taught him to do. He would negotiate with them, and he would win.

The one thing that he endlessly agreed on with his father was keeping the company safe and free from liabilities. That meant different things to different people, but the bottom line was that the company was family, and no one was allowed to hurt his family. If they did, he would come at them with all the venom a rattlesnake possessed and strike at their throats until they were dead. Those were the negotiations that James was sent on. They always brought in his particular set of skills and expertise near the end, when it seemed like a negotiation was going down the toilet. The board would bring him in and by the time he walked out, the company was back to sitting pretty and dominating every market that they had a stake in.

Now, James had three hours before his plane landed, and he planned on getting some rest. These business deals took a lot out of him. The negotiations alone were taxing. If only everyone could just agree to do things his way from the start, it would make life much easier. James reclined in his seat, took a sip of his bourbon, and once again closed his eyes, enjoying the silence. Once the wheels hit the ground, it would be time to get back to work, and moments like this would be hard to find. Negotiations weren't always easy and this specific one he expected would be no different. But he would come out on top, like they taught him to do.

CHAPTER SEVEN

Nova

It had been over a week since she ran away from police custody. It was hard to say how many days had gone be exactly, as any type of routine was out of the question. Not having a real destination in mind, Nova picked a direction and just kept at it. Eventually she made it out of the city, but the endless walking was taking a toll on her body. Blisters covered her feet, and her shoes were constantly soaked with sweat and rainwater. Seeing as how none of this was planned, Nova barely had anything for survival on her. Her bag contained two sets of clothes, stolen toiletries, hardly any money, and snacks from the motel. Nova didn't want to stop anywhere that first day to stock up in case someone noticed her. She kept her head down, hair in her face, anytime someone walked by her. Terror was constantly running through her already worn-down body and mixing with the adrenaline coursing through her veins.

Nova had been on the move since she ran, never staying in one place for long. She would walk until it felt like her legs were going to fall off, and then another hour before she would let herself have a small rest. Sitting down was never a problem, but standing back up was when she felt like her body was giving up on her. Forget finding somewhere to sleep a full night. Any small noise or whisper on the wind was enough to keep her awake in fear, and she would once again start walking, trying to escape it all. Her mental health took a beating in those days, becoming more paranoid and terrified with every step.

But she finally made it to a point where she knew that if she was going to make it any further, she was going to need supplies. Actual food, some type of shelter, more cash so that maybe she could stay in a motel room with a bed and a shower. She had already learned that sleeping under a bridge wasn't the best idea, when she had a run in with a few men that had taken an interest mostly in making her share whatever she had, whether or not she wanted to. Nova managed to get away unharmed the first time, but it was enough of a scare for her to tell herself never again.

Nova could not keep warm with the clothes she had, shaking especially during the night. Her fingertips and toes were constantly going numb, and her arms ached from the way she kept them wrapped around her body so tightly, trying to keep every ounce of warmth from leaving her. It was shocking that she hadn't already come down with some type of sickness, with her body worn down and the conditions she was putting herself in, but Nova knew she was walking a fine line. Something would have to change.

It had been raining off and on for days, but that final night, once the sun went down, the sky opened up and poured, washing out any hiding spots she could rest in. Her feet were sore, her joints ached, she was starving and chilled to the bone on some back road that had seen no traffic in hours. Her eyes were starting to see things that maybe were there, or maybe they weren't. Unable to distinguish what was real and what was in her head meant that she couldn't stay on the road any longer. She had enough sense to understand that, at least.

Just as her legs were about to give out, Nova saw a sign in the distance that lit a fire under her. Even over the wind and rain, she could hear the squeak of the old sign as it constantly turned, lit with neon lights, letting her know that there was a motel within reach. Somewhere warm and dry that she could stay at. She would have to use her debit card, which she had been keeping inside her bra for safety. Using it was risky. Nova didn't know who was hunting her at this point. The cops maybe, or her parent's killer, and using a bank card seemed like a bad idea. But the alternative was staying outside in the rain and the cold for yet another night, something Nova knew she wouldn't survive. She was already pushing her physical limits to the brink, and because of it, she had finally developed a bit of a chesty cough. If she wasn't careful, it would turn into something worse, and she could end up unable to defend herself.

As Nova got closer to the motel, she was running through the funds she knew she had in her head, wondering what would be better -taking a sizeable chunk of money out or just using her debit card whenever she needed it. Nova didn't fully understand how technology worked, so she figured if she only used her debit card sparingly, it would be tougher to track her. Tougher, but not altogether impossible. However, with the condition that she was in, she would have to take the chance.

The outside of the motel wasn't anything special; it looked like your average cheap motel on the side of the highway. A rundown exterior with rips in the awning, but the lights were on, and the sign said vacancies were available. It was enough for now. At least it looked clean. That was something to be thankful for.

Stepping into the motel lobby, soaked and frozen, Nova was surprised it wasn't as run down as the outside appeared to be. There wasn't much to look at, it wasn't anything fancy, but there was a rack with brochures for the nearest towns, as well as an ATM and a snack machine. Nova's wet shoes squeaked as she walked across the floor. The clerk behind the desk had his head buried in a chemistry book, looking harmless.

"Excuse me?" She hadn't spoken to anyone in days, and the strain on her throat was noticeable. The guy barely looked up and grunted at her in a way that said, "What do you need?"

"The … sign says you … have a room?" It was phrased like a question and the guy just nodded at her.

"Can I rent one for the night?" The guy sighed as he pushed his school-books away. A college kid working after hours for some extra money. He helped her out without even making eye contact, which was all the better for Nova. If he didn't look at her, he wouldn't see how horrible she appeared. He typed away on a computer almost as old as her before grabbing a key from behind him.

"Room Eight. It's forty dollars for the night." Nova just held up her debit card, and he pushed the debit machine her way.

"The diner across the street is closed, but it opens first thing in the morning. Same with the gas station beside it. The only other option is the snack machine behind you, but it only takes cash." As she was paying for her room, she made a mental note of the ATM by the door. She could get some cash and pick up some necessities from the gas station across the highway.

Once the debit transaction went through, the guy- Andy, his name tag said- handed her a small set of keys.

"Here you go. When you step out of the office, turn left and you'll find your room. Check out is 11 a.m., no exceptions unless you pay for another night prior to 11 a.m." Nova nodded, just wanting him to stop talking so she could go lock herself away for the night in a room with actual walls, a roof, and a deadbolt.

This seemed like a cozy enough spot to rest for the night, to refresh herself, and to plan some type of route, or at least figure out a destination. She couldn't run forever. Nova turned and let herself out of the office and Andy went right back to his schoolwork without giving her another thought. Walking three doors down, Nova found Room Eight and let herself inside.

The room itself looked a lot like the room the police had put her in. Small bathroom off to the side, bed in the middle, and it all came with a bit of a musty smell. Nova had to tell herself not to be put off by any of it. She was out of the rain, in a room with a lock, and no one in the world knew where she was. This was the best position she had been in for days now. That statement stuck in her head. No one in the world knew where she was. Not one human knew where to find her. It was both comforting and depressing when she thought about it.

Closing the door and locking not only the deadbolt, but the chain across the door as well, Nova still didn't feel quite right. There was a side table off to the side that, with shaky hands, she moved in front of the door. If someone wanted to get in, it may not stop them, but the noise of them bumping into it could help her be aware of the intruder quicker. With that taken care of, and all the curtains on the windows pulled shut, Nova made a dash to the bathroom to relieve her bladder. Peeing in a bush or a ditch while looking around to make sure no one was looking had gotten old fast. When she was done, she turned the shower on as hot as she could get it. Peeling her wet clothes off, Nova took the time, while the shower was warming up, to hang each article of clothing up to dry. Everything probably needed a good wash, but Nova could only do so much with her limited supplies. Nova stepped into the hot shower, feeling the steam and the heat burn her skin, and thought it felt amazing.

There was a small soap set on the counter that she brought into the shower with her, and as she scrubbed her skin raw, the lilac scent from the soap transported her back into the past.

Nova was just a little girl at the time and her mother was putting her to bed for the night. When she bent down to tuck Nova in, Nova got a whiff of lilac from her mother's shampoo.

"Mama, what's that smell that's in your hair?" She looked up at her mother with adoration and love.

"What you're smelling is lilac, and it happens to be my favourite scent and flower." Her mother sat on the edge of the bed and brought the blankets up around Nova's shoulders, helping her feel safe and snug in the bed.

"Do all people smell like lilac?" Her mother laughed.

"No, not everyone."

"Then why do you smell like it?" Nova asked, curiously.

"I like to surround myself by it because, to me, it smells like a calm day in the garden. Now go to sleep, my girl." She kissed Nova on the cheek and told her to go to sleep.

"Mama? To me, it smells like you. Like Mama hugs and kisses." She smiled at her mother and closed her eyes.

Coming out of the memory, Nova noticed the shower was cooling off. Tears streaked her flushed face as she stepped out onto the cool floor. How she would ever feel safe again, Nova didn't know. Her parents were her world, and they were gone. Feeling safe and loved was gone. Now she was an empty shell, and she felt like she would crumble with the smallest wind.

Nova wasn't under the shower long enough to fully get rid of the chill in her bones, but it had helped a great deal. She mentally noted that having a long, hot bath before she left might help her better. After drying off, Nova took a few moments to run some soap and water over her sad selection of clothing, leaving out a few pieces to sleep in. Once that was all done, and once she double checked the locks and the windows, Nova finally climbed into the bed, hoping for an actual sleep.

That night was no different from any other and unfortunate the nightmares were back and wouldn't let her get more than an hour or two of sleep at a time. A few hours after her shower, Nova gave up on sleeping and tried the bath, hoping it would ease some of her physical pain from her travels, and it did. So much so, in fact, that she fell asleep in the tub.

An hour later she woke up, thrashing, convinced for a moment that she was still fighting a wolf for her life. Calming herself down took some time. She got out of the tub and tried to cuddle on the bed under the sheets, but she soon realized that she wouldn't find any more sleep here. The rain had ended, and the wind had died down. Seeing no other reason to stick around, Nova packed her things. First light wasn't far off and by the time she hit up the ATM, she should be able to buy a few things at the gas station across the street.

Looking into the mirror in the bathroom and taking in the way her face had thinned out, the dark bags under her eyes from lack of sleep and lack of good nutrition, Nova absently wondered if she would ever get a full night's sleep again. Or would her nightmares chase her into an early grave?

CHAPTER EIGHT

Nova

Walking up to the check in desk, Nova scolded herself. This was the third motel in a week. Worn down, Nova knew she shouldn't be spending her money that fast. It wasn't going to last and there was no way she was going to be able to keep this up much longer. But she was more than exhausted, sleeping less than two hours each night before the dreams started. She kept telling herself that, even if she wasn't sleeping, just being in a safe room with a lock on the door and a roof over her head was worth the expense. Unsure if it was helping her paranoia or feeding it, she just couldn't turn up the chance every time she spotted a motel in the distance.

Her dreams were a constant issue, nightmares that were getting worse with each passing night. It didn't matter if she slept with the lights on, lights off, if she put a chair in front of the door or not, if she had a warm shower before bed or not. It did not seem to matter at all. No matter what she did, the nightmares would come. The dreams changed slightly from night to night. Nova wouldn't always start off in the cold basement. Regardless of how it played out, though, it always ended the same. It always ended with her dying, and then waking up screaming only a few hours after she fell asleep. This night was no different. Nova fell asleep holding the remote from the crappy television in the corner and all the lights in her room on.

On this night, her dream started off in a library. Nova was wandering around, trying to find a specific book despite not knowing the title. She looked through stacks and stacks at all sorts of titles. None of the books looked right.

Just as she relaxed into the dream, a growl started off in the corner. She hurried her feet up, still looking through the books. Inside she felt as if she was getting closer, but the closer she came to finding the right book, the louder the growling got. Chills went down her spine and she could taste bile in her mouth. Her fear making her hands shake and her breath coming out in pants. This wasn't the first library dream, even though they all looked slightly different. Still, every time she would have this dream, she would get closer and closer to finding the book before a wolf would appear from behind the stack. It would get close enough that she could see the drool falling from its mouth and the light glint off of its teeth before it would lunge at her and clamp its jaws over the top of her throat. She had tried everything, running away never worked, and neither did trying to fight the wolf off.

No matter how she reacted to the wolf after it appeared, the dream always ended the same. The wolf would lunge, attach its jaw around her neck, and she would wake up in tears and covered in sweat, with her heart almost beating right out of her chest. Some nights, she could still taste the bile in her throat. Other nights, it would take hours to get her hands to stop shaking in fear.

Nova was exhausted, physically and mentally. She was finding it hard to distinguish between what was real and what wasn't. Everything was bleeding together. Confused at whether she was waking up from a dream or falling into one, her days and nights were bleeding together. There were moments during the day where Nova swore she could hear the growling following her from place to place, while she was wide awake. She would look around corners with fear in her heart and any time she was around other people, she kept her head down and shuffled as fast as she could past them.

A couple of people tried to ask her if she was alright, her appearance giving off junkie vibes, but Nova couldn't find it in her to ask anyone for help. That growl kept getting closer and if she didn't keep moving, it would finally catch up with her. Nova didn't want to know what would happen if she could no longer outrun the wolf.

The worst part was knowing that she was losing touch with reality and not being able to do anything about it. Logically, her brain was trying to tell her that there wasn't an actual wolf following her. If there was, it would have been spotted by other people, and if an actual wolf was following her, it wouldn't be taking days or weeks to attack her. But to Nova, that growl sounded so real, so close, and so terrifying. It vibrated down her spine daily now. She had tried to ignore it, tried to not let it bother her, tried to move her feet faster and faster as if that would help, but her body had a mind of its own and the terror would flood her veins without her permission. Nova knew she couldn't go on like this forever and she was right.

Nova had planned on picking up a few supplies the next time she found a small convenience store on the edge of any small town, as they usually asked no questions despite how she looked and acted. This day, however, everything changed. Nova ran out of luck, and she found herself in a situation she could no longer run from. The gas station on the edge of town had apparently closed down some time ago, if she took it's run down condition as proof of anything. She had to venture further into the town to stock up on water and something to cure the gnawing hunger pains in her stomach. It must have been a weekend because, the closer to the centre of town she got, the more she saw people out and socializing in the streets. Nova was trying to make her way through the growing crowd without being noticed when the growling started following her again.

For a moment, Nova told herself there was no way a wolf was hiding in this crowd without being seen. But panic crept in at an alarming rate. Nova could not control it as she kept looking around frantically while pushing her way through all the people. She stopped trying to be polite about it, shoving people as they got in her way and looking behind her constantly.

The growling was getting closer and closer, drowning out the shouts of those people that she pushed to the side. It no longer felt like a figment of her imagination. Nova was sure an actual wolf was following her. How did no one else see it? Why was it after only her? She had to get out of there; she had to run.

But where could she go? There was nowhere that she felt safe, not even in her own home. Her heart was racing so fast that she felt like it would explode. Was there no sanctuary to be found? Nova's mouth had gone dry, and whimpers had come out of her throat. Was there no one that could help? She could feel the snap of the wolf's teeth on her ankles as she fell to the ground. The surrounding people looked on, backing away to give her space. They were confused about what was happening with the poor young woman while silently judging her for having some kind of adverse drug reaction.

None of that mattered to Nova as she tried crawling away on her hands and knees. She started hysterically shouting out at everyone.

"Leave me alone! Help me! Someone help me! The wolf! The wolf! He's here!" No one was listening, no one was helping. Nova curled up as tight as she could in a ball on the ground, rocking back and forth, constantly muttering about the wolf between her sobs. The crowd started growing bigger, but no one took a step forward to help. Pity and judgment were all she saw when she looked at the faces, as if they all knew it was hopeless for this poor girl.

Nova had never been so lost in her life. There was no map to help her find her way, for she was lost in her head, in her own mind. She became so lost that she didn't notice the cops show up, or the paramedics. So lost that she didn't notice when they drugged her to keep her from hurting others or herself. So lost that she didn't notice as they transported her into the ambulance. And so lost that she didn't notice when they put her under a seventy-two-hour surveillance hold at the local psychiatric hospital.

CHAPTER NINE

Haven

Haven went to visit her grandmother a few days after her last visit, but if she was being honest, she wasn't in the best place for the visit. She's had a long day at work; she hadn't been sleeping well, and she had considered skipping the visit. It's not like Betty would notice if she didn't come and Haven hadn't been spending much time on self care. A quiet day at home in her pajamas sounds so appealing, until that familiar pang of guilt hit her gut. The pang of gut that had her feeling like a bad granddaughter.

Betty would have scolded her for feeling guilty, but Haven couldn't help the feeling every time she wanted to change her plans to visit. The woman practically raised her, was at every school event, every recital that Haven asked her to be at. Not once did she ever cancel on Haven, not once. Betty was there for everything when Haven was growing up, good days and bad, and not once did Betty ever complain about it. Haven had dozens and dozens of memories of her grandmother being there, always for everything. It was those memories that had Haven walking through the doors at the institution yet again, storybook in hand, instead of taking the day off.

When Haven got into her grandmother's room, she was in for a pleasant surprise. Betty was not only awake, but she was sitting up, extremely lucid and chatty. Betty rarely had a full understanding of her surroundings, even on her good days. Instantly, Haven's mood improved, and she was happy that she hadn't simply stayed home. If she had cancelled like she had wanted, she would have missed this, and moments like this were worth their weight in gold to Haven. When Betty saw Haven, her entire face light up even more.

"Haven, my dear granddaughter, what are you doing in such a place?" Betty had such a smile on her face and beckoned Haven over with her arms out wide, waiting for a hug.

"I came to read to you." Of course, Haven obliged her and hugged her a little harder, not believing she was having this moment. The last lucid moment was well over six months ago. In an instant, Haven felt like a child again, embraced by her grandmother's warm arms.

"Nonsense, child. A young woman like you should live experiencing adventures, not reading them to an old bat in the crazy ward." Haven knew then that not only was Betty lucid, but she knew exactly where she had ended up. Part of Haven's soul died at the knowledge that Betty knew things were bad enough that she had been committed for her own good.

Haven also didn't have the guts to tell Betty just how little adventure her life had. Haven wasn't big on the dating scene, and she didn't exactly have many friends outside from work colleagues. Her life was simple, just like Haven, and she was okay with it. Growing up, Betty had always told her that adventure would find her one day, and to make sure she never let the opportunity pass by. But so far, adventure hadn't come calling for Haven.

"You know I enjoy doing this. You read these to me so many times growing up, it's my turn to read them to you." Haven pulled the chair closer than normal, not wanting to be far from Betty while she was in such a good mood. Haven noticed her face was getting sore, but she could not stop smiling. She realized just how much she had missed her grandmother, despite visiting her weekly. It just wasn't the same. Betty looked at her granddaughter with nothing but love and adoration.

"How about a little conversation first? Tell me about how things are going with you?" Not one to turn down anything this woman asked for, Haven spent the next half hour talking to Betty, the real first talk they've had in a long time. They laughed at little inside jokes and Betty ate up every word Haven spoke.

Just as Haven was picking up the book to read, she glanced outside at the orderlies rolling someone past. The book almost fell from her grip as she looked at the woman's face. There was no way she would ever forget that face. It was the woman from her dreams. The woman who was always getting attacked by the wolf. Haven's heart dropped into her stomach as she dropped the book on the floor. Without registering it, Haven stood up and made her way to the door. The orderly pushing the bed with the unknown woman had stopped at the nurses' station just outside of the room for a moment. Haven stared at the woman, confused as to how she dreamed about someone before ever meeting them. Had she maybe seen this woman before in the halls? Haven rubbed her eyes for a moment, making sure that was she was seeing was real.

"New transfer. Where are we setting her up?" Haven heard the orderly talking to the nurse about the patient. If she was new Haven wouldn't have seen her before. Was she being paranoid about this?

"Help her, Haven." Betty's voice came out in a harsh whisper from behind her. Haven whipped her head around to look at Betty, who's eyes were filled with panic as she looked past Haven to the young woman.

"Help her." Betty's voice was becoming stronger as the air in the room became chilled, causing goosebumps to go straight down Haven's back.

Looking back at the woman for a split second, Haven turned back and made her way to her grandmother. When she was close enough Betty, with a strength Haven didn't know she possessed, reached out and grabbed Haven's arm tightly.

"Ow, Grandma, let go. You're hurting me." Haven tried to pry her fingers off, but for a tiny, elderly woman she had quite the grip, and Haven didn't want to actually hurt her grandmother.

"Help her! They are coming for her!" Betty's eyes were wide and frightened. Never in all her time visiting the institution had Haven seen an episode like this. It scared her and she couldn't tell if she feared her grandmother, or for her. There was a gnawing at the back of her mind, something trying to tell her to pay attention, but the entire situation was confusing.

Still trying to get her arm away, Haven looked back out the door to see the orderly wheeling the woman away. Looking back at her grandmother, Haven slowly tried pulling her arm away, with no success at freeing herself. If she couldn't sort this out, she would need to get the attention of one nurse so they could medicate her grandmother.

"That woman, she needs you!" Betty was sitting straight up as her voice started getting louder and more hysterical. The veins in her neck started straining at the effort she was making. Betty started saying the same thing repeatedly. It was almost like a scene right out of a horror movie. Something had possessed her grandmother and Haven was at a loss for what to do.

"Just relax, Grandma, you're working yourself up." Haven started looking for the call button on the bed. This was obviously more than she could deal with on her own. The nurses' station wasn't that far away, but with the new patient arriving the nurses were occupied. There was no guarantee that anyone would hear her.

"Now! Help her now! She will die without you!" Her voice was no longer a whisper but came out of her like a megaphone. The strength and desperation in her grandmother's voice was enough to slam her back against the wall, out of her grandmother's grip. She seemed almost possessed, and the voice that came out of her was not her voice. It was strained and yet it had power behind it. The monitors in the room all started going off, and the nurse ran in as Betty had trouble breathing. Three different nurses came flying in to assess the situation as Haven pressed herself against the wall.

"What happened here?" the nurses yelled to Haven over the sound of the machines. Not really sure herself, all Haven could do was shake her head back and forth. Betty kept fighting the nurses, trying to get over to Haven, trying to get Haven to listen to her. The lead nurse took charge, barking an order at the other two, asking for medication to calm Betty down.

"Betty, I need you to calm down. Betty, I'm going to have to give you a sedative to help you relax. You're putting too much strain on your heart! What did you say to her?" Two of the nurses started restraining Betty to the bed, as the third gave her a shot of a mystery clear liquid and then glared at Haven as if she caused all of this.

"Nothing! She had a lucid moment, and we were just talking about the old days." Haven was holding her arm close to her chest, rubbing the spot where her grandmother had held her tight. Still in shock over what was happening, Haven tried replaying the last half an hour to make sure she did nothing to cause this.

Betty was proving to be resistant to the sedatives, so the lead nurse started shooing Haven into the hall.

"I need you to clear the room until she is settled. Wait for me at the nurses' station, please." Haven took one last look at her grandmother, who hadn't taken her eyes off of Haven, and then ducked out of the room as the lead nurse closed the door for privacy. Haven's wobbly legs got her to a chair right beside the nurses' station and she shakily took a seat. Her heart was beating so fast and nothing but concern for Betty clouded her thoughts.

That was so strange! Who was her grandmother talking about? Haven looked down the hall. And it was only then that she remembered seeing that woman being wheeled by the room. Was it the same woman from her dream? The same woman that just went by on the stretcher. It couldn't be, it just couldn't! It had to have been a coincidence, though that was just around the time Betty started losing touch with reality again. Could all of it be connected? Haven knew that in her dreams that woman was always being hunted. But she had never mentioned those dreams to Betty. Haven waited for a few more minutes, her thoughts spinning round and round, until the nurse came to see her, holding Haven's bag and jacket in her arms. Haven stood up to meet with her.

"I'm sorry, she's not up for any more visiting today." The nurse looked apologetic enough that Haven believed she meant it. Haven grabbed her things from the nurse and tried to look into her grandmother's room, but it was obscured as the blinds and door were shut.

"What happened to her? She's done nothing like this before." Haven couldn't get the sick feeling out of her stomach. Something wasn't right, that wasn't the grandmother that she remembered raising her. Never had her grandmother so much as raised her voice at Haven, and she would never raise a hand to her. The spot on her arm where she was grabbed started throbbing, as if to remind her it was there.

"I can't be sure. It's possible that it was just the excitement of seeing a family member while she was lucid. If she remembered who you were, that would have meant something to her. It may have just overwhelmed her. It's tough, I know, with dementia patients. Everything can change in an instant, and they can go from their regular self to someone unrecognizable. It's traumatic to witness." The nurse started making notes in Betty's chart, acting like the entire incident was nothing out of the ordinary.

"I've never seen her do anything like that before. I've been with her from the start, and I've never seen her act that way. Does this mean the disease is getting worse?" Haven couldn't help the tremble in her voice. If the disease was getting worse, and agitating her heart condition, Betty wouldn't be around for much longer.

"It's possible that this was just a one-time thing, but you should get yourself prepared in case it isn't. The strain that she put on her heart today was very serious. If she has more moments like this, it could cause more damage to her heart. Something she may not overcome." The nurse looked up and saw the concern and despair on Haven's face.

"Look, she's lucky to have you. There are so many people in here that will never get a visitor, let alone a regular visitor." Haven couldn't imagine leaving her grandmother, the only family she had left, to rot in a hospital bed and to never see her again. The thought alone was almost more than she could bear. Unexpectedly, that thought brought the poor woman on the stretcher to the front of her mind.

The nurse continued on- "Don't let this stop you from visiting. Even if it seems like she's never going to be herself again, you should still come by. It's important for not only her, but for you too. Spend as much time with her as you can, while you can." Haven wasn't exactly listening to everything the nurse was saying, but the overall sentiment was getting through to her.

"I plan on it. She's all I have left. I won't let her be alone, even if she doesn't know I'm here." The nurse smiled a reluctant smile at Haven, as if she didn't believe what Haven was spouting. Haven couldn't blame her, either. The nurse probably heard that from families every day and yet most of them never came back. That young woman's face popped into her head again. Did she have a family? Would someone be visiting her? Why couldn't she get that girl out of her head? Haven stood there for a second, debating whether she should even ask something, before she threw caution to the wind and did it, anyway.

"Can I ask you a question? When someone is admitted here, how long would it be before they would be allowed a visitor?" The restraints on the young girl's wrists flashed into Haven's mind. Perhaps she wasn't here by choice. If that was the case, would Haven even be allowed to visit her? A lot of the employees may well know her, but the rules still applied to her. The nurse thought about it for a minute, as if trying to calculate what Haven's motives were.

"It depends. Every case is different, every person is different. A seventy-two-hour hold is placed on someone when they are first admitted, like your grandmother, for observation and safety. After that, it changes on a case-by-case basis. Your grandmother was allowed visitors after that because we could keep her heart stable and her moods were always delightful. Someone in a more drastic situation may have to wait a week or more before we feel they could benefit from outside visitors" The other nurses coming out of Betty's room gathered at the nurses' station and Haven took that as her cue to leave.

"Thank you. And thank you for taking care of my grandma. I'll be back in a couple of days to see her again." Haven slowly walked out and to her car. With one last look at the building, Haven got in the car and made her way back home.

Once she got there, Haven went about with her regular nightly routine. She made a light dinner, prepared for work, watched some TV and changed into her pajamas before bed.

But no matter what she was doing, for the rest of the night Haven couldn't help but to think of that woman. There were so many questions that she needed answered. Why was her grandmother so interested in the young woman? Was it just a coincidence? Was it really because she was overwhelmed? Or was there a deeper meaning to all of it?

More importantly, how was she dreaming about someone she had never met, but then seen a day later? Haven had once heard that all the faces of the people in your dreams were from people you had seen during the day. The brain was spectacular and could remember a face it had only seen for mere seconds in a crowd. Was that where Haven had seen that young woman before? Or was it more? Was the universe trying to prepare her for something? Or was she simply reading far too much into it? One thing was for sure, Haven wouldn't be getting much sleep that night. As she closed her eyes, she thought of how scared her grandmother had been. Rubbing the spot on her arm as she fell asleep, Haven could have sworn she heard a low, quiet growl from the corner of her bedroom.

Chapter Ten

Haven

The next morning came too early for Haven, who was having a hard time getting out of bed. She had hit the snooze button twice before rolling over and opening her eyes. Staring at the ceiling, Haven was still trying to piece together everything that had happened the day before. From her grandmother having a lucid day, to the strange woman on the gurney, all the way down to the mystic message from Betty. Haven was shaken up most of the night and sleep did not come easy.

Glancing at the clock and noticing the time, she had to get ready for work. Work: that was another situation causing her sleepless nights. While she hadn't said anything to her grandmother about it, work wasn't going as well as Haven had let on.

Haven had only been with the company for half a year, making her still fairly new. Working in the mailroom wasn't her goal, but she needed to increase her income to help her grandmother's medical bills. She didn't talk to many people there, and she found they acted like she didn't exist.

The job itself was pretty easy, and it came with significant benefits, but Haven was convinced a monkey could do her job. It didn't really fulfill her and if she didn't have her grandmother to think about, Haven wasn't sure she would have stuck it out for as long as she had already.

Haven had to observe a certain order in the large company. The mailroom was pretty much at the bottom of the power totem pole. Just walking through the halls to her desk in the early mornings was enough to have her hackles up, so to speak. Some of the people that worked in the office seemed almost dead inside. They would come to her to get projects printed off, but it was as if they were dead behind the eyes. Haven couldn't put her finger on it, but something was off with them. The longer she worked there, the more she felt that corporate corruption was a valid concern.

Her coworkers were always ducking in and out of off limit rooms at odd hours. At times, she had to send out couriers to discreet locations to retrieve packages she was not allowed to handle, and no one could mention it once the object had been delivered. There would also be employees that seemed to disappear off the face of the earth out of nowhere, and no one ever said anything about it. Haven could think of three separate people during her short term of employment who were around for the planning and meetings, but then they disappeared. If she had listened to her gut, Haven would have left that company in the dust ages ago. Rent had to be paid and bills had to be taken care of, so Haven stayed until the company gave her a reason to leave or something better came along. Picking up her I.D off of the counter on her way out, Haven stared at it for a minute and asked herself the same thing as the day before, was it really worth it? Despite all the adult reasons to keep a job, was the misery worth the paycheck? Coming to the conclusion that, at least for the day, the paycheck overruled the misery, Haven opened her door, stepped out, and headed off to work.

As she was walking into work that morning, her mind was occupied with thoughts of her grandmother's condition. Betty was getting worse. There was no denying it at this point, and there was no way to know how much longer she had left. The entire episode the night before wasn't sitting well with Haven, either. Betty had looked terrified and almost possessed. Haven had gone over and over every detail of their visit and still did not know what had set her grandmother off.

Haven was not paying attention, tea in one hand, lunch bag and purse in the other, and collided with a wall. A wall that turned out to be a man in a suit. A suit that was now, because of her, covered in tea. Shit.

"For Christ's sake, doesn't anyone watch where they're going around here? Well, what do you have to say to yourself? You just poured hot tea all over my designer suit!" Mortified was not a strong enough word for what Haven felt when she realized what had just happened. Standing in front of her was none other than James Hunter, the son of the CEO of the company, and someone that was known for his temper.

James had interns thrown out for little to no reason, and Haven just spilled tea on his designer suit. The air left the room and Haven wanted to vomit from nerves. Not knowing how to proceed, she stood there, stunned, stumbling for something to say. And true to his reputation, James started getting enraged, more and more with every moment that Haven could not form an actual response. Finally, after he had turned three different shades of red and steam was pouring out of his ears, Haven found her mouth.

"Sorry! So sorry, sir! I'll pay to have it dry cleaned!" In her mind, she knew she didn't have the money to get it dry cleaned, but she would have to figure it out. She would have promised him her first-born child if it would have calmed him down. They were drawing a crowd. Whispers from coworkers as they skirted around what was happening. He growled at her offer and stepped forward, getting into her space.

"What good does that do me now? I have a meeting in five minutes with the mayor, and now I smell like a goddamn cup of chamomile tea!

Not to mention the physical pain I'm going through, what with burning liquid practically thrown at me, and all because of your reckless behaviour. Do you need some type of training? Do they not show you how to walk with your head up while you're carrying a hot liquid in whatever pathetic department you work in? What department do you even work in?" James towered over her, backing her into a wall. Haven's words kept getting stuck in her throat and she felt like she was back in grade school on the playground, being pushed around by the biggest bully for existing.

"My name's Haven. I work the mailroom and print room." Haven squeaked out as she could barely get the words out. The knowledge that he had enough power to get her fired for something like this kept circling round and round in her head. She hadn't got to know anyone yet. No one had her back. She was expendable, and in a company where people disappeared, being expendable wasn't what you wanted to be known for.

"Ha! Isn't that just the way life goes? On my way to a meeting worth thirty million dollars of work over a two-year term, and the frumpy mail room girl is the one that becomes my downfall." He spat his words at her, as if she was a pile of filth. The veins in his forehead even made themselves known as his entire face remained one angry shade of red.

One bystander handed him a stack of paper towels and he snatched them away without even acknowledging someone had helped him. Haven put her hands up in front of her, as if she was attempting to calm a feral animal. If she didn't get away from him quickly, she would end up in tears. It wasn't something that she could control, but whenever she became upset, embarrassed, or confronted with something, she would cry. The last thing she wanted to do around James was cry. She couldn't imagine what that would do for her.

"Again, I'm really sorry. I didn't see you coming around the corner." Tears welled up in Haven's eyes, yet she fought to keep them from falling.

In her mind, she was already packing up her belongings and looking through the want ads for a new job so that she could make rent next month and keep her grandmother in the facility.

"Haven't you done enough already? Just get out of my way!" With that he stormed away, leaving Haven's heart beating abnormally fast and unshed tears brimming over her eyelids. The group that had gathered around quickly dispersed. Not one of them dared offer her any kind of sympathy, knowing that if they were caught comforting her, it would be their hide pinned to the wall.

Haven ran into the closest bathroom she could find, camped out in one stall, and silently let the tears fall until she could calm herself down. Public humiliation and terror weren't something that she had signed on for when she took this job. If there was one thing she couldn't handle, it was getting yelled at, especially over an accident that could have happened to anyone. Being able to handle conflict was not her strong suit. She could read about strong-willed women in all of her favourite novels day in and day out but when it came down to it, she just didn't have it in her to have the same type of backbone, the same guts that her favourite characters had.

For the rest of the day, Haven refused to leave her desk, keeping her head low to keep it from being blown off. She heard James shouting and stayed in her office rather than risk going out while he was there. Haven even went as far as skipping lunch, choosing to snack on the one granola bar she found at the bottom of her purse. Anything to keep her at her desk and away from that monster.

When the end of the day finally came, Haven shut her workstation down and practically ran out of the office. When the elevator opened, she was ready to jump on it, only to see it wasn't empty. James Hunter stood there, staring at her like she was a moron, waiting for her to get on. Haven's feet were glued to the ground. Not even an earthquake could make her move as all the blood in her body turned her face an unpleasant shade of red.

James huffed at her and pressed the door close button, scowling at her until the elevator shut and moved on. The tears once again started collecting in her eyes. She was ready for the day to just be over. If it wasn't already a Friday, she would have called in sick the next day. This really was not her week. With everything that had happened with James, Haven had forgotten all about her grandmother and the girl at the institution. At least, until she fell asleep that night.

Chapter Eleven

Jax

Across the country, two young men worked as fast as they could, in silence. Six computer screens surrounding them, with many city maps, news articles, and software displayed that the average person wouldn't understand. Both men kept their fingers dancing across keyboards, gathering up information and putting it all together in a variety of files. The work they were doing was never to see the light of day, and the person they were working for was just as mysterious as the project that they were working on.

The two men had identical faces, yet their style of clothing couldn't be more different. The man on the left was dressed like a surfer who had gotten lost on his way to the beach. He had on a plain t-shirt with the logo of the local surf shop, along with a pair of blue board shorts. His ensemble was complete with a pair of beaten-up sandals, and his sandy blond hair was tied in a bun at the back of his head. His face was cleanly shaven, and his crystal blue eyes looked more like contacts than natural.

His identical twin was wearing a much more roguish outfit. He was wearing a dark wash pair of jeans, paired with a tight fitting black long sleeve shirt. Completing his look was his pair of black, slightly tarnished motorcycle boots, and the black watch band around his right wrist. His hair, or what was left of it after he had shaved half of his head, flopped to one side. His left ear was full of earrings, and they weren't his only piercings. He also had one in his left eyebrow, the right side of his nose, and the left side of his bottom lip. What wasn't showing were the tattoos that danced up both of his arms and across his shoulders.

Other than the clicking of the keyboards silence surrounded them for hours on end. Day in and day out this was their routine, until the man on the left finally let out a yip of excitement as he threw his hands up in the air. His brother merely glanced over at him, not even bothering to take his fingers off the keyboard. He just waited for the update he assumed was coming.

"We found her! Better get him down here. He's gonna want to see this." The man on the right took a quick glance at his brother's screens before reaching over to pick up his cell phone. He typed up a quick text, sending it and nodding to signify that the message was sent. He then went back to scanning his brother's screen, absorbing the information he saw there before finally answering his brother.

"He'll be pleased. He's been in such a shit mood lately." Both men nodded in agreement. While they understood the emergency, the last few weeks had been filled with nothing but sour moods and time running out.

"He'll be happy to see we both have something for him. Apparently, there is another player in the game now, and she may change things slightly. Come here and look at this." Both men crowded around one computer screen to go over what looked like security camera footage from another unknown place. It wasn't long before they heard the door slam open from behind them and the heavy footsteps hurrying across the floor towards them.

"What's the story? Someone talk to me." A slightly smaller in stature man sauntered into the room, rolling the sleeves up on his worn-out dress shirt as he walked. The contrast between the dark floral print and the stark white suspenders holding up his brown wool dress pants was jarring. His black, slightly wavy hair fell in front of his eyes while light freckles dusted across his nose.

"Well, we may have stumbled upon something quite special here, boss." After looking at the monitors in front of both brothers for a mere minute, he stood back and put one hand on the shoulder of each twin.

"I knew it. I could feel it. Things are starting to turn our way, the vibrations coming off of the earth are different now. Boys, we found more than her. We finally found the way to tip this battle into our favour." The twins looked over at him, relieved that they could finally be helpful and find what he was looking for.

"What do we do now, Jax? Should we get them?" The man just shook his head, the glow of the monitors reflecting in his eyes.

"We have a lot of preparation to do. Don't worry, Watson, those girls will make their way to us. It's our job to be prepared for when they do finally arrive. Let's kick it up a notch, Walker, and get this place ready for company. It's time to set the stage for the greatest battle of our lives." And with that, he ran back through the door he came in. Both twins turned back to their monitors, printed off the information they had there, and then took off out the door, following their boss.

CHAPTER TWELVE

James

What a fucking idiot! Twice in one day he was forced to interact with the lowest of low, the most pathetic wallflower at his company. The fuckin' mail room girl, not even someone with talent, but someone who ran errands for the talent of his company, had effectively ruined his day.

Earlier in the day, after she dumped an entire cup of tea onto his very expensive suit, making him smell like the inside of a teapot, he had to hustle back to his office to put on his back up jacket and shirt. It wasn't something that he had planned for, which meant that he had to rush in order to make it to his meeting on time. James hated being late, especially when he was the one that called the meeting. Experience taught him that people didn't want to give you millions of dollars to do a project if they thought you were lazy or incompetent. Being late made him look unorganized. It made him look weak. He was not fucking weak.

In the end, he had to do some wining and dining to get the mayor on board, but by the time the meeting was over, the project was theirs for the taking. James could even talk the mayor into upping the price by a million.

That had made his day more bearable, at least until he ran into that fucking mail girl in the elevator. She had the gall to just stand there and stare at him with that blank look on her face. He didn't have time for that. Didn't she understand that twice in one day she held him up from a meeting? He didn't feel like sticking around to see if she would eventually pull her head out of her ass and get on the damned thing, so he closed the doors and the elevator continued on down.

After closing the doors, James pressed the one button right beside it. It was no different from any other button, except it didn't have a number or a pictograph on it. It was very plain, but only a handful of people knew what it was for. The elevator eventually stopped, and James exited, making his way to the security doors. He pulled out his access pass, the only way to open the door, and slipped through. On the other side was a large steel door, the last precaution in case someone accidentally made their way down here.

It was time for him to check in with his special ops team to see if they had a new target, a new business deal for him to make.

James walked to the end of the hall and let himself into the research room. There were three rows of desks filled with the most up-to-date computers and at each computer sat an employee whose sole job it was to provide him with locations and details about his targets. These employees spent every moment of everyday tracking people down, learning their routines and every deep, dark secret they had. They knew the layout of each target's house and place of work. They knew it all; it was their job. If they ever failed their job, they were quickly "ended" and strangely enough, they were never heard from or seen again.

Past the three rows of computers, against the far wall, were two giant screens. On one screen, there was a list of ten different people, their names and corresponding pictures. Seven of those names were crossed out with

red, while the three remaining were staring back at James, a constant re-
minder that he may have been making progress, but his job was far from
over. In fact, he fully expected that list to grow even more while his people
tracked down the last group of targets.

The second screen had a map of the city dead centre, with a variety of
foreign city maps along the edges of the screen. Each map was used to track
not only targets, but any informants, anyone of use that could help make
his job easier, and anyone who could make his job a living hell.

As James made his way into the room, he was handed a tablet full of new
information, anything collected since early that morning. Most of it was
pretty meaningless, it wasn't up to him to decipher different patterns of
his targets, but he looked over every single piece of information, knowing
that anything could be the piece of information that helped his hunt.

From the looks of it, his team may have found the next target on the list.
That could be a pleasurable distraction while he waited for the one that
got away to pop back up on their radar. The tension in the room eased
slightly as his team noticed he was pleased with the information they found
for him. Speaking to no one specifically, but the room as a whole, James
addressed them.

"Good. This is at least something. I'll check it out. The only thing that
seems to be missing is the info I need on the missing girl. By the time I come
back in here, I want information on that damn girl."

With that, he let the threat hang in the air, turned around, and left as
each worker started doubling their efforts, knowing the next time James
came in that room either they handed him the target's head on a platter, or
it would be replaced with one of theirs.

CHAPTER THIRTEEN

Jax

"Boys, tell me we know more." Jax came storming into the computer room. Walker turned to him and handed him a file folder. While Jax flipped through it, Watson summed up everything he was looking at.

"Haven Summers is a twenty-three-year-old woman. Grew up in a quiet neighbourhood. She is the only living relative of one Betty Conners. Her parents passed away at a young age and Betty became her legal guardian, raising the girl. Haven went to her local community college before finding work at a fairly well know multi-billion-dollar corporation. She works in the mail room and has for a little less than a year. Nothing abnormal about that, except for the fact that the place that she works apparently is being run by the Hunter family." Jax stopped looking at the file and glanced over at Watson, furrowing his brows as if he was trying to figure out a puzzle, and when it clicked Jax looked pissed.

"Shit. No, no, she can't be one of them. She's the one we've been looking for." Jax put the folder down and glancing at the screens in front of the twins, looking for an answer.

"Before you spiral, just listen. I don't think she's aware of who she's working for. She works in their mailroom and in her spare time she does the most old lady shit that I've ever seen. She doesn't have a social life and, other than visiting her grandmother regularly, she doesn't really go out much. I wouldn't be surprised if her favourite hobby was fucking knitting." Walker started pulling up a few files on the computer.

"So, what, the one person on this planet that we need to turn the tides just happens to coincidentally work for the enemy, with the enemy completely oblivious of who they have in their mailroom? Come on, we're not that lucky!" Jax tilted his head to understand the logic he was being presented with. He may not have known these guys for very long, but they were good at what they did, and if something caught their attention, then it must have been for an excellent reason. The other side of that was that if they felt something or someone was innocent, then they probably were.

"Pretty much. The company itself is corrupt as fuck, but it doesn't appear that Haven is a part of that at all. With a company as big as theirs, it shouldn't be a surprise that they don't know snuck in right under their noses. It even took us a bit of time to find her, and we've been looking for what, months?"

Jax looked slightly unsure, so Walker piped up.

"Jax, we don't even know if they're aware that someone like her still exists. We only started looking because we ran out of options, but if they think her kind are extinct, they would have no reason to search for her." The twins were making sense, and as much as it drove Jax crazy, he knew he had to trust their judgement.

"That's not all, though. We found something else. Something that you're not gonna like." Watson started pulling up new information on his screens.

"What am I looking at?" Jax leaned over Watson to read the different reports as quickly as they were appearing on the screen.

"Look at this clip." Watson brought up security camera footage and pressed play. At first, it didn't look like anything out of the ordinary. It was a dark and deserted street except for a woman walking quickly towards the camera. She kept looking behind her, as if she was worried someone would see her.

"Okay, I don't get it." Jax saw nothing suspicious about this, but an eerie feeling came over him. Something bad was about to happen on camera.

"Just wait." And sure enough, as he said that, the woman turned down an alley just before the camera. Jax was about to question it again when he saw what the boys were talking about. It was quick, and to the untrained eye it wasn't anything, but Jax saw it. The lady turned into the alley and a split second later, the reflection of a bright flash hit the bricks of the building. While the camera didn't actually reveal what the bright flash was, the woman did not come out of the alley after that. The boys searched through twelve hours of footage to be sure, but there was nothing. It was as if she disappeared into thin air.

Watson then walked Jax through the other three pieces of footage that they got, and on each one someone could be seen fleeing the scene of a murder, only to disappear down an alley, followed by a reflection of the flash of something. Watson then brought up numerous articles describing how these murders were all sitting unsolved because of the lack of evidence and lack of suspects.

"Shit. Shit. Shit." Jax started pacing back and forth, running his hands through his hair.

"Tell me it's not what I think it is." Both men looked to Jax for confor-mation.

"We're running out of time. They are finding our people faster than we can. We can't stop, though. We have to keep going. Okay, here's what we're gonna do. Watson, I want you to dig deep, go back as far as any written text has gone, and make me a complete list of potentials. I want to know how many are out there, where they all are, who they are, everything you can. I don't want to be blindsided by these murders anymore. We need to get ahead of them, get there before the company does. Walker, you keep searching for footage like this. If this is the company killing our people, if this is what we are looking for, then those girls are in more danger than they know. I need to know every detail of every murder. Time of day, location, any scuffs on the sidewalk. I want to know it all. There has to be a pattern, and we needed to know it yesterday. It's only a matter of time before the wrong people piece together what we know about Haven Conners. The moment that they do, those two girls are going to have nowhere safe to hide."

Jax looked at the twins, his enforcers, the only two men he trusted with his life. Their eyes were bloodshot, their faces pale. Jax had been pushing them a lot lately, and it was wearing them down. Between the research and the training, training that they were doing in their downtime with what little downtime they had, they were going to burn out if Jax pushed them much more.

"I know it's a lot. You guys are already putting everything into this, but it's not enough. We need to keep pushing, at least for now. We can't afford to stop or relax. Haven can't afford for us to slow down now." Jax felt horrible for what he was asking, but one look at either Walker or Watson told him everything he needed to know. They weren't objecting, they weren't fighting what he was saying. They were preparing, mentally they were calling on their energy reserves and preparing for the long haul.

"Jax, we get it. We've lost far too many already. Haven won't be one of them. Nova won't be one of them. We'll get back to work." Walker did his best to reassure Jax that they were there to work, to help.

"I agree. We've got this, boss. But, uh, do you think you could order a pizza or start a pot of coffee? I feel a long night ahead." Jax gave Watson his best half smirk and nodded. He was grateful he found these men when he did.

"Of course. Alright, get to work. You know where to find me if anything new pops up."

Walker stopped him for a minute.

"Have you had any luck yet? Is she responding at all?"

Jax shook his head.

"Not yet. But I'll keep trying. It helps me monitor her. Who knows, maybe she'll reach out on her own. If so, I'll be there. For her, I'll always be there." And with that, Jax left the room, and the twins got back to work.

CHAPTER FOURTEEN

Nova

Nova woke up in an extremely white room. Waking up wasn't the right phrase. It was more like Nova's brain refocused its lens, and her surroundings became more and more clear. When she came to, she was lying on a bed with very simple surroundings. She went to sit up, only to notice that someone had strapped both her hands and feet to the bed. A mild sense of panic came over her as she tried to break free. The door opened and in walked a short, round nurse with a clipboard.

"Hello dear, don't mind me, just here to check on your status." Nova could tell she was a kind lady by the way she talked and the way she carried herself. But none of that did anything for the rising panic bubbling up in Nova.

"Whe—" Coughing, Nova's throat felt full of gravel. It took her a few moments to clear it as best she could.

"Here, let me get you some water before you try again." The nurse put a straw from her pocket into a small bottle of water that she pulled from her other pocket and held the straw to Nova's lips. Water felt cool going down her throat, and Nova couldn't suck it up fast enough. After Nova got a good drink in, the nurse pulled the straw away.

"There you go. Now what was that?" Nova cleared her throat again and then, once more, tried speaking.

"Where am I? And why am I strapped down? Can you take these things off?" Her voice was still gruff, but the more she talked, the easier it was getting. However, she was still tied down and Nova started struggling against the bonds that kept her down.

"You're in Red Ceaders, Miss. The straps are for your protection, as well as the staff's. I'll have the doctor come in and evaluate if you still need them." Nova looked at the nurse, confused. Why wouldn't the staff be safe around here? She would never hurt anyone. The name of the place also didn't sound familiar, and a small part of Nova knew she wouldn't like the answers she was about to get. The nurse must have seen the confusion on Nova's face.

"Do you not remember when you came in, Miss?" Nova shook her head at the nurse, furrowing her brows, trying to bring back any memories from the past few days, but everything was still foggy.

"I'll get the doctor. She can fill you in and answer questions you have." The nurse quickly exited the room. Nova tried to remember how she had gotten there. Everything was fuzzy and her memories would only come to pieces. The door opened and in walked a middle-aged woman in a white coat with a stethoscope around her neck and a weathered look to her features, as if she had seen a lot and nothing would surprise her.

"Hello there. It's nice to see you're awake. I'm Doctor Thompson. I was told you had a few questions for me, but let's start with your name. We went through all the belongings that you had, but you had no ID on you." She seemed nice enough, but slightly standoffish. Nova noticed the doctor was waiting for her to answer.

"My name is Nova." Her voice slightly shook with fear. "Why am I here, and why am I tied to the bed?" That was all the information Nova was willing to give her until she got more answers. Her brain was trying to piece together the situation, and some things were just not sinking in for her.

"Well, Nova, you're here because the police brought you to us. You were having some type of episode, and we couldn't seem to calm you down. How much of that do you remember?" Doctor Thompson stood ready for more answers, making notes in her chart every so often. Small pieces were coming back to her. The motel rooms, the constant walking, and her constant fear. Not ready to have that discussion with a stranger, Nova kept it simple.

"Not much. I hadn't been sleeping much before. Please, doctor, why am I strapped down?" The doctor made a few more notes and then looked at Nova, trying to assess how much of what she was saying was true. The doctor decided that the no nonsense route was the way to go.

"Nova, when the cops found you, they couldn't get you to calm down. You were shouting about being followed and you were curled up into a ball on the ground. They had to sedate you to put you in the ambulance. By the time they brought you here that had worn off and you were having another episode, but this time you were lashing out and anyone that got near you. We had to sedate you and restrain you so you wouldn't hurt anyone, including yourself. Do you remember what you were shouting about?" Nova took a moment, letting all of it come back to her. Every agonizing detail flooded her brain. Her parents were dead and there was someone coming after her.

"The wolf." It came out as a whisper, as if she was afraid that suggesting such a thing out loud would materialize her nightmare in this very room.

"Yes, that's what you keep mentioning, but who is the wolf, Nova?" Nova stared down at the floor, refusing to make eye contact. No one would understand. They were all going to think she was crazy. If she hadn't lived through all of it, she, too, would think it was crazy. The best thing to do was to stay quiet. At least that way, no one could mock her or make fun of her for it.

"You can close yourself off all you want, but that's not the way to get out of here. This isn't the first time we told you why you were in here. We've tried it a few times, and every time we do, you have an episode and need to be restrained. Obviously, something very traumatic has happened to you. You need to tell me what that was if you want me to help you." Nova just shook her head. They wouldn't believe her, no one would. She might as well be prepared for a long stay in here.

"You can't help me. No one can help me. I tried running, but that didn't work. Now I'm stuck in here and he'll get me. I will die in here, and there isn't anything anyone can do about it." Her voice cracked, but she said it, anyway. And that was the last thing Nova said to the doctor. The doctor tried for a few more minutes but Nova refused to respond completely, instead choosing to stare at a spot on the wall. Doctor Thompson finally had enough, told Nova she would be held until she started co-operating, and left the room.

Nova stared at the wall, knowing for certain that her time was up. She didn't run far enough, or fast enough. She wasn't quick enough and now she was a sitting duck. A single tear ran down her face. The ache in her heart for her parents continued to grow. This was what broken felt like.

CHAPTER FIFTEEN

James

James was sitting in his office, looking at the view outside his window. The sun was going down and the streetlights were going on. Everyone down there was running around, living their lives, not fully understanding everything about the world that they lived in. He was getting impatient. His team was taking far too long finding the information that he needed. When his phone rang, his only thought was that this better be the lead he was hoping for.

"Sir, you should come down here. We may have found something." Gregory, the team lead, said. Saying nothing back, James slammed the phone down and practically ran to the elevator. The trip to the basement seemed to take forever. By the time the elevator doors opened, James had composed himself.

When he stepped off the elevator, they were already waiting for him at the doors to the meeting room. James stormed into the room, pushing past his workers and grabbing the tablet out of Gregory's hands.

"This better be good." He scrolled through the information quickly, picking up keywords and locations and putting the puzzle together in his head. With the flick of his wrist, everything he was looking at on the tablet appeared on the screen at the front of the room, including a sizeable picture from a motel security camera of the target that got away. It was grainy, not the best quality, but he could tell it was her in an instant.

"She was electronically off the radar for a while, which is why it took so long to find anything. But last week her debit card was used in a few different places. It took some time, but it looks like the trail was actually leading this way. Now the card hasn't been used in a few days, but now that we know her pattern, all we have to wait for is her to use the card again and she should be no more than an hour's drive away." Gregory stated. Without provocation, the corners of James' mouth started lifting up in what could only be described as a predator's grin.

"One more purchase and then she's mine." James was happy with this news, thrilled. Looking at a picture of the young girl, James chuckled. Even through the grainy picture, it was obvious how unwell she was doing. Going on the run wasn't easy, and while she led his team on a bit of a chase, it was time to end this and bring her in.

"I want you checking every security camera a hundred miles around where this was taken. She is nothing, a nobody, and there is zero reason we shouldn't have already caught her. The only thing I can say is she's been damn lucky. That luck ends today."

His team took a second to look at him before they all jumped back to work, shouting to each other, breaking the map up into quadrants and assigning them to each other. They would find her before the weekend. He guaranteed it.

James slowly walked up to the screen while everyone resumed work around him. He took a good, long look at her.

"Come closer, little lamb. It'll all be over soon." With that, James turned around and left the room, silently planning all the ways he was going to make her pay for using up so much of his time and resources. Of course, once his team had her, she wouldn't be leaving the building alive, but not before he had his fun, that was for sure.

Chapter Sixteen

Nova

It's an awful thing, being trapped in one's head with nothing but the memory of finding your parents brutally murdered. At some point, the drugs wore off, but by then Nova was resigned to whatever fate had doled out for her. Anything that would take away those horrible images was welcomed. The doctor tried conversing with her every day, but with no reaction from her, the conversations were short and one sided. Since she hadn't tried attacking anyone since her first night, and she had not tried to hurt herself, the restraints on her wrists and legs were taken off and Nova was given socializing privileges.

Nova saw it for the strategy that it was. She could ignore the doctor every visit, but if she wanted to eat in the cafeteria and sit in the common room, instead of spending all of her time locked away in her room, Nova would have to be around others. She would see the nurses' side eye her, checking to see if Nova chatted with any of the other patients. Sometimes that was all a patient needed, was to be around like-minded individuals who were going through similar issues. It helped some open up, and once they started talking, they were more open to discussing heavier topics with the doctors.

Nova rarely took these opportunities, going as far as refusing to leave her room for days at a time. The doctor didn't let that dissuade her and made it mandatory for Nova to spend at least one hour a day outside of her room in one of the common areas. She couldn't make Nova talk to anyone, but she could stop Nova from completely locking herself away.

No matter how much she wished and prayed she would just evaporate into thin air during socialization time, an orderly would come into her room, help put her into a wheelchair, and then wheel her out to the common room. Nova's body had given up on living, leaving her legs weak and unwilling to hold her up. It was as if all the strength in her body had simply disappeared, and movements as small as moving a spoon from her bowl to her mouth was almost more than she could bear. If someone was going to kill her, what was the point of trying to extend her life? She was completely hopeless.

On this day, they placed Nova right beside an elderly lady, both pointed at the small television along one wall. The orderlies figured that the two of them would be no trouble at all, and maybe it would make for a quiet and laid-back afternoon. What the orderly didn't know, what Nova didn't know, what even the hospital administrator didn't know, what that it wasn't, the orderly that placed her beside this woman. It was fate.

The elderly woman was in her own wheelchair with a soft pink and white blanket laid across her lap and a light-yellow cardigan hanging from her shoulders. She was watching an old, animated movie on the television while another group of women were gossiping beside her. The elderly woman looked over at Nova and it was as if a light went on in Nova's brain as she felt a powerful urge to talk to this lady, an urge she couldn't explain. Weeks had gone by without her socializing. Despite this, Nova mustered a small smile for the old lady. The old woman smiled back and took that as a cue to visit.

"You seem young to be in here. What troubles you, my dear?" Nova could barely move her head, let alone talk. The urge she had felt to connect with this lady was trying to fade. Nova had hoped this woman would do what everyone else around her did once she refused to talk to them—leave her alone. It was just too much work, too much energy to make the effort. The women who had been gossiping beside them stopped what they were doing and, not so subtly, were watching the conversation.

One lady spoke up while the others looked on. "You won't get much out of that one, Betty. She's been out of it since they brought her in. Refuses to talk to anyone, even the doctor." The air of superiority was thick amongst the group, but Nova just didn't have it in her to care what these women thought of her. It surprised her to hear the bite in Betty's response to these women.

"What do you even know about it?" Betty instantly snapped back at them, and Nova noticed the venom in her voice. Betty appeared to be unhappy that they were trying to gossip about the new girl right in front of her face, and a small part of Nova warmed to the elderly lady for it. The women apparently didn't know how to read the room, as they continued to share Nova's story without her permission.

"Haven't you heard? She's the wolf girl. Freaked out right in the middle of downtown. Screaming bloody murder about someone being after her. Poor thing, she's been through a lot. It's no wonder they strapped her to the bed at first. A real loony, that one." The head of the gossip circle appeared eager to share anything she knew and hoped someone else would pipe up with even more information. From the look that Nova saw on Betty's face, she was filled with disappointment and disgust at what was taking place.

"Yes, thank you, Iris. Once again, you proved all you are good for is eavesdropping information that is none of your business." The group of ladies sat up in shock at the rudeness coming from Betty. "You ladies keep walking until you find something useful to do with your time. This young thing is none of your business." Betty scoffed and shook her head as the gossipers got up and walked away. Lowering her voice a little, she leaned into Nova, who stared at her wide eyed.

"Quite the busy body that one. The lot of them, actually. Believe they deserve to know everyone's business. Hmph. Garbage if you ask me. What goes on in a person's life is no one's business but their own. That's my motto." If Nova had the energy to smile, she would have loved to. This elderly lady was quite something. For the rest of the afternoon, Nova sat there with Betty, listening to her many stories about life and letting Betty explain the different movies that appeared on the television. Not once did Nova talk back, but that was alright with the both of them. Nova could see that Betty just wanted someone to listen to her and Nova just wanted something that would get everyone else to leave her alone. In each other, they found the solace they were searching for, at least for a short time.

CHAPTER SEVENTEEN

Haven

It was a humid night, and the air conditioning in Haven's building wasn't as reliable as she would have liked. Haven was never good at sleeping in such heat, and when she did, her dreams were always stranger than ever before. This night wasn't any different.

Instead of one fluid dream, this time it was more like snapshots or clips of the mystery girl that had been showing up in Haven's life. The clips went fast, but at the end they would loop around and start all over again. This time, Haven was the one going through the terrible events, not just watching them from afar.

At first Haven was walking down a hallway to a closed door in a house. She knew that there was nothing good behind that door, could feel it in her gut, but she couldn't stop herself from pulling the door open. What she saw there made Haven's stomach heave. There was blood everywhere. On the walls, on the bed, and on the floor. Two dead bodies, a man and a woman, looked to be brutally attacked by someone or something. Haven felt an odd emotional attachment to these victims, but before she had a moment to think about it, she was off to a different place.

Next, Haven found herself in a police car, arriving at the police station and being led into a room by two officers and a detective, where she was questioned about the murder of her parents. Haven stuttered her words, trying to tell the officers that she was in the wrong place, that she didn't belong here, but they either didn't hear her, or they didn't care. The questions kept on coming, as if they thought Haven was the one who committed the crime.

That turned into a small hotel room with a cop car parked outside. Haven was sitting on the bed, rocking back and forth. Chills went up and down her spine, her mouth dry and her eyes sore from crying. She was alone in the room but had the distinct impression that she was being watched. It would have been easy if Haven could just get up off of the bed and walk out the door, but her legs wouldn't move and she was stuck on the bed, in fear for her life.

The next three snapshots came upon Haven quickly. First, she was running down a cold alley in the middle of the night, looking behind her as she kept telling herself to just keep moving. Next, she was hiding under a bridge, slinking back into the shadows to hide from the drunk stumbling by. It wasn't enough, and he spotted her. He started making obscene gestures at her as he advanced upon her.

In the blink of an eye, run, Haven was in a crowded shopping square, where she could hear the snarl of a wolf right behind her. She couldn't see it, but she could feel the breath from its putrid jaw on the back of her neck. As she turned around to run, she was admitted against her will to an institution. That scene felt all too familiar to Haven, though she didn't have any time to wonder why it felt so familiar. Haven was physically on the gurney, being rolled down the hall, but when she looked around for help, she looked into one room along the way. For a split second, the world spun as Haven stared back into her own eyes from inside the room. It was as if she found herself looking at her own reflection, but it was only for an instant before she was wheeled away.

The last scene in the sequence was one that was fairly familiar to her by this point. Haven was standing in a forest in the dark of night, and there was the dreaded wolf standing in between her and freedom. The only difference this time was that she was standing face to face with the wolf. With every growl and snarl, the wolf grew bigger and finally, as if someone let go of the leash, the wolf lunged at Haven. As it came for her, she would turn to run and she would find herself back in the hallway by the closed door, knowing that whatever was on the inside of the room would make her want to vomit.

Haven went through this dream sequence three full times before she understood what was happening. As if a light bulb was suddenly turned on in her brain, she woke up, opened her eyes, sat straight up in bed and understood what she was seeing. She was seeing through the eyes of the girl from the institution. She was reliving whatever this girl had gone through, the weeks that led up to her being admitted to the same institution as Betty. Haven sat there in slight confusion for a bit. How was she getting all of this information? Was it simply her overactive imagination, or was there more to it?

Haven wanted to believe that there had to be a reason she couldn't get this girl out of her head. But no matter how much she went over every detail, nothing jumped out at her, nothing that explained what was happening. Why was she seeing these very intimate, horrible moments, moments she could only assume were memories that didn't belong to her? It was all in the past, except for the dream sequence in the woods, which meant there was nothing she could do about it. She couldn't prevent any of it. The girl was already institutionalized.

Giving up completely on getting any sleep, and wanting answers, Haven grabbed her laptop and started researching the details of her dream. She opened up her search engine and looked for any news stories on a set of murders that may have happened in her town. The faces of the victims looked old enough to be her parents, so Haven inferred they were these girls' parents. When she couldn't find any that matched the description that she saw in her dreams, she widened her search parameters to towns close by.

It took a few hours, but she finally found a news story from a few towns over. A young girl had come home from college to find her parents murdered in their own home. She was taken into police custody, and that was the last time anyone in town had seen her. Somehow, she had slipped right through their hands and, until just a few days ago, appeared to have fallen off of the face of the earth. There was a picture of her with a plea to the public. If anyone had any information, the police were asking to be notified. Haven choked on her own spit as the face of the girl at the institution, the girl haunting her dreams, was staring back at her from the newspaper article. Right underneath the picture was her name: Nova.

The absolute horrific things that Nova must have been through and must have seen. Haven didn't understand. Why hadn't Nova told anyone her name? While the article had answered a few of her questions, it also just brought out more questions, and there was one thing Haven could think of to do to get more answers, but it seemed so simple. Haven could just visit Nova at the institution, if she was allowed visitors.

Setting her laptop down, Haven took a minute to really think it out. This wasn't territory that she was used to. Getting in the middle of a murder investigation, inserting her into Nova's life when Haven didn't even know the state of Nova's mental health. This could all blow up in her face easily. It would be easy for Haven to simply back off right now.

She wouldn't have to get involved. It wasn't her job to befriend this girl. It really wasn't her job to solve a murder, or to help to police track Nova down. Really, it hadn't taken her that long to discover the truth. What excuses did the police have for not knowing anything?

Although, if she didn't at least try, Haven wouldn't be able to live with herself. Maybe she could just go talk to the girl, see what she had to say. That would be that. She would then tell the police where this girl was and then she could move on with her life. That would be how she could help. A pit was forming in her stomach and a small voice in the back of her head told her she wouldn't be able to simply walk away at that point. If she was going to insert herself into Nova's life, she wouldn't be able to just let the girl suffer and fade away. Taking a deep breath, Haven looked outside.

The sun started coming up and Haven realized she had spent her entire night dreaming about Nova, and then researching her. Her alarm clock went off, telling her it was time to get ready for work, but Haven knew there was no point in going in today. There was no way she would be useful at work with the lack of sleep and all the questions floating around in her head.

James' face flashed in her mind, cementing her decision to stay home for the day. The last thing she wanted to do was to have another run in with that jackass on top of everything else. Haven quickly called in sick and decided to use the day to get some answers. Hopefully, by the end of the day, she'd be able to sleep peacefully, and the mystery of Nova would be put behind her. After a quick shower and a change of clothes, Haven jumped in her car and waited in the parking lot for the institution to open its doors to the public.

CHAPTER EIGHTEEN

Haven

The moment the clock turned over to 9 a.m., Haven jumped out of her car and practically ran to the front door of the institution. When Haven walked in, it surprised the usual staff behind the window to see her. She almost never visited this early during the week, most often than not Haven was an evening visitor.

"Good morning, here to see your grandmother?" the nurse at the desk asked her as she walked up. Haven could go one of two ways here, she could say she was there to see Betty, only to wander the halls once she gained access, or she could tell the truth and hope she had enough pull to gain access to a stranger.

"Yes, I had the morning off and figured I could use more time with her." Haven responded, lying through her teeth. The nurse didn't think anything of it and gave her access. As Haven was walking through the halls she was trying to nonchalantly look into different rooms, looking to see if she could find Nova. But by the time she was outside of her grandmother's room she still hadn't had any luck. Taking a quick look around Haven couldn't see anyone really paying her any attention, so she went down the next hallway, hoping some kind of sign would just appear to help her out.

Just as she was peeking into yet another room, a voice surprised her from behind.

"Excuse me, what do you think you're doing?" Haven jumped around to find the head nurse for the floor staring at her with a look that told her she had one shot with her excuse before she was getting kicked out.

"Oh, hi. Sorry, I was, uh, just looking for the ... bathroom?" Haven internally cringed at how pathetic she sounded. She couldn't come up with anything better than looking for a bathroom? Every nurse on this floor knew her face and how often she came, did she really think the bathroom excuse was going to work?

The nurse crossed her arms and raised an eyebrow at Haven. The gig was up, there was no point in lying anymore. Haven took a deep breath and prayed that this nurse was at least somewhat reasonable.

"Okay, yeah. Lame excuse. Okay, here's the truth. I was looking for someone that's new here. I don't have her name, but I saw her the other day, and I just wanted to see if she was ok."

"Anyone new to the institution needs to have their visitors registered at the front, you know this. Snooping around random rooms is a big confidentiality breech. We expect you to know better, given how often you're here visiting Betty." Haven felt like she was a teenager again, being scolded for breaking curfew.

"I know, and normally I have nothing but respect for the rules, especially here where you take such good care of my grandmother. But ..." The nurse rolled her eyes.

"But you were hoping just this one time we could break the rules because of how well the staff already knows you?"

"Um, yes?" There was a reason Haven always followed the rules growing up; her stomach was in knots, and she already choked vomit down twice during this conversation.

"Nice try. Now you can either go and visit Betty, and only Betty, or we can find someone to escort you out of the building." Dejected, Haven backed away from the nurse and started towards her grandmother's room.

"I'll just go visit Betty. Sorry about that." Haven turned and walked to just outside Betty's room. The nurse followed her to make sure she was going to the right room, but just as they started approaching Betty's room, an alarm from another room started going off and the nurse took off at a jog down the hall, and around the corner.

"Psst." Haven turned around and saw one of the newer nurses at the nurse station that sat outside of Betty's room. Haven smiled at her and stepped forward.

"I hear what you were saying. You were looking for the Jane Doe that showed up a few days ago, aren't you?"

"Yeah, I know it's against protocol, but I just wanted to check in on her." The nurse nodded and then quickly scampered around the station to stand next to Haven.

"Do you know her?" the nurse questioned her.

"No, not really. I know, it's a breech in protocol. I was already told." The nurse waved her off.

"It's against protocol, yes, but follow me anyways." The nurse started speed walking down the opposite corridor and it took Haven a second to realize she was supposed to follow. She caught up to the nurse.

"Are you sure this is okay? The other nurse told me no, and I get it. Rules and all of that." The nursed kept looking around as she led Haven to just outside of a closed off room.

"I had a younger sister. When she was fourteen, she had a full psychological break, and no one in my family could figure out why. That was ten years ago. Dozens of doctors and a variety of medications, and nothing helped. Year after year she wasted away in a place like this until she was a shell of her former self. In the end, her heart gave out on all of those medications, and we lost her. Nova looks a lot like her. I couldn't help my sister, but maybe I can help Nova. I just hope it's not to late for her. She won't eat. She won't talk with the doctors. Multiple nurses have tried, and failed, to get any kind of reaction out of her, and everyone is coming away empty handed. Everything, aside from severe medication, has failed. There has been one moment where I've seen anyone make an impact on her, and that was when she was sitting beside your grandmother. From time to time, we have been known to buddy patients up with fellow patients in order to aid them in their recovery. Obviously, with Betty's mental state, we don't want to put any more on her than we need to. But, since you're Betty's granddaughter, maybe you'll have some luck. Now I can't give you long, maybe five minutes?" the nurse explained while her eyes filled with tears. Haven was taken aback by the emotional story and had to swallow the lump in her throat before answering the nurse.

"I'm sorry that happened to your sister ... I promise, I won't be long," she croaked out. The nurse looked around one more time before cracking the door open and ushering Haven inside.

"Thank you!" Haven whispered before turning around and taking in the room around her. It took Haven a second to get her bearings. The room was bare, nothing but an iron bed frame and an old mattress with the thinnest of blankets on top. Bars on the window and a dim light on the ceiling helped make the room look like a prison cell. It looked nothing like her grandmother's room. There was nothing warm about it, nothing friendly.

After taking in her surroundings, Haven sought Nova and found the poor girl sitting on the bed, staring blankly at the floor. Haven entering the room didn't even phase her. Nova looked so lost and so hopeless. Her long red hair was slung over one of her shoulders in a tangled mess. The pale and partially sunken in face was probably caused by her refusal to eat. Her eyes had no light behind them.

There was a chair placed across from the bed. More than likely, they bolted it to the floor. Haven waited a moment to see if Nova would acknowledge her presence at all, and when there was no communication or movement from the bed, Haven made her way over and sat on the chair. Haven cleared her throat slightly, not wanting to startle the girl but desperately trying to get her attention.

"Uh, hello there." Haven waited for a beat, but nothing came from the girl on the mattress. Haven wiped her sweaty palms against her jeans, not sure what movements to make to get Nova's attention. They were running out of time before Haven would be kicked out by the nurses. If she was kicked out before she was able to connect with Nova, Haven knew she wouldn't be allowed back in this room, and that was unacceptable. The best way forward was to be straight with her.

"Ok, look, we don't have a lot of time. You don't know me, and there is no reason for you to even listen to what I have to say, but I'll say what I came here to say and then leave you be, if that's what you want." Again, Haven paused, but the girl on the bed didn't even bat an eyelash to her.

"My name's Haven, and even though you've never met me, I just wanted to make sure you were okay. I don't know what's going on, but I feel like the universe is almost shouting out to me, telling me you need my help with something." Haven swallowed harder than she would have liked, the words falling out of her mouth were drying it out at an alarming rate. She should have brought a water bottle.

"Of course, that sounds crazy, why a complete stranger would come into your room and offer to help? It's nuts, but I can't seem to get rid of this feeling, and so I figure the only way to move past this is to come in here and talk to you. None of this makes sense to you. I sound crazy enough to be put in here, no offense." Haven internally winced as she realized what she had said.

"I promise I won't make this a regular, everyday thing. If you tell me right now that you don't need my help with anything, if you tell me right now to never come back, then I will walk out that door and leave you alone." Haven stopped for another minute and took a deep breath. This was harder than she thought it would be. Talking to a wall would have been more productive at this point. But Haven had to keep trying. It wasn't in her to give up just yet.

"But if you need something, even something so small that you don't think it's worth asking for, I would like to help you with that." Her words turned softer, and she stared at Nova, trying to will her to say anything at all. Holding out a hand in friendship to a complete stranger wasn't easy, however Haven couldn't imagine how hard it must be to be where Nova was, to live through what she lived through, and then to be open enough to admit to a complete stranger that she needed help. Haven could appreciate the battle going on in Nova's brain right in that moment. Haven just wished Nova would look up and see in her eyes that Haven was here to help. A few heartbeats later, it's as if the battle in Nova's brain had finally made progress as Nova's eyes flashed up to connect with Haven. It was only for a moment, but the amount of emotion that Haven felt in that moment was staggering. The heartbreak, the loss, the absolute panic and fear. It was like a punch to the gut and Haven had only gotten a glimpse.

"Do you need help? What's your name?" Haven wanted to make sure things were done on Nova's terms, telling Nova that Haven knew all about her was the wrong choice at that moment. Nova needed to be in control of the meeting. That meant keeping some things hidden from her, at least for a little. The silence in the room was almost suffocating. Haven gave it one last try to see, and if she still got nothing, she would have to find a way back on another day.

"Look, I know they put you in here for a reason, and you've probably had enough people walking in here, asking you all sort of personal questions, treating you like anything you say doesn't make sense, but if you want to talk, I'm here." Haven waited for a few more seconds and when nothing happened, she figured Nova would not take a chance on her.

"Stupid fairy tales, crazy grandmothers ..." Haven started muttering to herself on her way to the door. Right before she reached for the knob, she heard the smallest, softest voice that she had ever heard. It was so little that she couldn't understand the actual words Nova said at first.

"What was that?" Haven asked, turning back to the girl. Nova hadn't moved much, but merely shifted her torso towards Haven and the door. Her eyes focusing just beyond Haven's face at the wall.

"Nova." Her voice came out like a cracked whisper.

"Nova?" Haven was so worried she wouldn't get anything else out of Nova, she almost held her breath, stood statue still, and tried to make sure nothing would spook her.

"That's my name. Nova, and I need help. Please?" Nova looked up and made eye contact with Haven. It wasn't easy, but she held that connection and wouldn't look away. Now that communication was open, Haven couldn't quite figure out where to go from there.

"What do you need my help with, Nova?" Haven had read somewhere that the best way to secure some type of trust was to use someone's name constantly in conversation. Slowly, she started making her way back to the chair and sat back down. All the while, Nova kept her eye contact. Tears started to slowly leak out of Nova's saddened eyes.

"Please don't let him get me. Please don't let him kill me." Nova's voice was hollow and lacked any confidence in the help she was asking for. Haven almost fell backwards with that statement. While Nova looked like she didn't have any hope left, maybe Haven could help change that. Haven noticed that, while Nova had made the first step, asking for help, it was almost as if she didn't believe it would come her way.

From her dreams, Haven knew something, or someone, was hunting Nova. If only she could get a name, she could warn the police. Looking at Nova's small stature and hearing her hopeless voice, Haven knew she had officially hit the point where she wouldn't be able to just walk away if things went south. There was no way she could, or would, just walk away from a human being that was this broken, without a hope in the world. Haven had to do something.

"Who's trying to kill you, Nova?" The air in the room was thick with the fear pouring off of Nova. Haven could see sweat forming on Nova's brow as Nova worried her hands back and forth, a sure sign of the anxiety hidden just beneath her skin.

"The wolf. It's okay if you don't believe me. No one else does. That's why I'm going to die." The tears that had started out as light picked up and they covered half of Nova's face, and yet it was a silent cry. Nova didn't wail, she didn't lash out, she just sat there, silently crying, as if waiting for it to all be over. As she leaned forward in the chair, Haven hated how utterly hopeless Nova sounded. Her body language wasn't any better. Nova sitting with her shoulders hunched and refusing to give any more eye contact.

"Nova, why do you think someone is trying to kill you?" Haven knew her time would be up soon. The nurses were pretty strict on visiting schedules on a good day. On a day where she had to sneak her way into a room, Haven couldn't see them giving her any extra time at all.

"I just know. Feeling him circling around my life, looking for an open spot to get me. I'm a sitting duck here, and I know he's on his way to finish the job." The more Nova talked, the less raspy her voice got. Nova was back to staring at a wall. It was something, but it wasn't enough. Haven needed more details, just something more to go off of. While she wanted to help, she couldn't keep every man on the planet away from Nova her entire life.

"Have you ever seen this man? What does he look like?" There was a pit developing inside of Haven. One that told her she wouldn't be ready for the answer to that question.

"I've only seen him in my dreams." Nova lowered her face once again, as if even talking about this man was causing her to curl up on the bed in fear.

"What does he look like?" Haven was leaning over so far in her seat that the slightest breeze would knock her onto the floor.

"He's a taller guy. Fairly fit build. Dirty blond hair, with a beard. His voice, though, that's the most terrifying thing about him. It's dark, and dirty with a rasp. He talked to me. Told me he was coming for me. He said—"

At that moment, the nurse walked in and told Haven that her time was up. It took the nurse a moment to realize that she had interrupted an actual conversation. While Nova had barely moved, she had turned her body to Haven and was willingly conversing with her.

"I have to go, but can I come back and visit you? More officially maybe? If you put me on your visitor list, I could come and we could finish this talk?" Haven prayed that the progress she made would be enough. Nova somewhat nodded and with that the nurse pushed her out of the room.

Walking down the hallway, Haven looked back at the door for an instant before finding her way back to the parking lot. That woman, that poor, terrified woman.

CHAPTER NINETEEN

James

This was the third meeting in a week with his team. They were flooding him with information and coming up with a strategy. They had traced the girl on multiple different security cameras, but it became clear early on that she didn't have a destination and she definitely didn't have a plan. She was running scared, which made it more difficult to determine where she would go next. James wanted to make sure he had multiple plans ready to go. Every detail mapped out, every "what if" covered. The last thing he wanted to be worrying about was the smallest detail that could go wrong or lead back to him and his company.

"Sir, we've got something!" James was beckoned over to a monitor in the middle of the room. James took charge of the computer, putting the information once again on the big screen at the front of the room. The information in question was a grainy video taken off of someone's phone. As it played in the background, more and more videos popped up from different points of view, all covering the same situation.

"We found this on a social media website. It looks like our girl had a mental break a few days ago and it was caught on someone's phone." The man whose computer James took over relayed to him. James was looking at a grainy account of Nova's breakdown, almost gleefully.

"Give me the details. What happened, and where is she now?" James demanded. He was just itching to finish up this transaction.

"She started really freaking the public out. Cops were called and then she was sedated and put into the back of an ambulance. From what my sources can find, it looks like she's still in custody somewhere." the man explained to him. James was watching the video and there was something strangely familiar about it. He knew those buildings in the background.

"Where did this all happen?" James asked. Every video played, constantly repeating over and over. He could hear the chatter of the crowd, but over all else he could hear Nova screaming about being chased by a wolf. James stood to his full height, proud of what he had accomplished so far with this target. Killing was easy, but to successfully create a hallucination that created this much fear in someone, that was quite something indeed.

"That's the market district." James froze, taking his eyes off the screen and looking at his team.

"Wait, our market district? Are you telling me she's been right under our noses this entire time?" The worker flinched a bit, but stood his ground the best he could, almost successfully keeping the tremble out of his voice.

"She's been committed against her will to the institution. She's only a few blocks away. Now, they had her under a seventy-two-hour solitary hold to evaluate her, but that's since been lifted." The techy pulled up security footage from the institution and it showed Nova being put in her room. James watched the footage for a minute and was about to turn away when something caught his eye. He had the tech replay a segment of the footage.

"That face right there. Can we zoom in to see who that is?" When the tech did it, James knew immediately where he saw that face before. The freakin' mail room girl. What was she doing visiting Nova in the institution? How did they even know each other? Their research showed that Nova didn't have anyone that would miss her. When did that change?

"Can I get in there unseen, into the institution?" James wanted to finish this tonight.

"No. Well, not yet. We're working on taking control of the cameras so that we can shut them off when we need to. They also have a security guard posted down the hall from her room, probably a formality. We'll need to arrange with the proper people something for that guard to be doing when you go. But at least for now we know where she is, and she isn't going anywhere, anytime soon." That did soothe James a bit, but it wasn't enough. He needed to know more. He hated she was so close.

Realistically, could he get in there and finish the job? Yes, of course he could. He was fucking great at what he did. But could he get in there without being discovered or seen? That was a chance that he couldn't take. Not with everything on the line. Either he waited until his team created the right moment, or until she was out of the institution. Either way, he didn't like waiting, and it put him in a foul mood.

On his way back up to his office, he couldn't get that scene out of his head. This mail girl better not be something that was going to get in his way. It would be better to know if she would be. Back at his desk, he pulled up her personnel file, making a few mental notes about her. He was memorizing her home address. It was time to have another chat with Ms. Sawyer.

CHAPTER TWENTY

Haven

Haven got back to her apartment later that night, head so full of questions that she didn't remember the drive home. It had been a long and strange day. She went to meet with Nova for answers and all she came away with was more questions.

Even with all the distractions Haven's body knew the moment that she crossed the threshold into her apartment that something was wrong. Every nerve in her body stood on alert, goosebumps running down her spine. Something wasn't right in her apartment. Her breathing picked up and Haven had the eerie feeling that she wasn't alone.

Leaving the door wide open, so as to not block herself in, Haven put down her bag and grabbed the first thing she could find, which was the very large and dense book of fairytales sitting on the counter beside the front door. She was going to bring it back to her grandmother, but put it down by the front door and forgot about it in her rush that morning. While it wasn't exactly a deadly weapon, it was heavy enough to knock anyone around a bit.

Tip toeing through her dark apartment she cleared one room at a time, all the while silently scolding herself for not backing out immediately and getting the landlord to walk through it with her. It was hard to see, but Haven didn't want to start turning lights on until she was sure there was no one there. The kitchen was clear, the living room was empty, and the bathroom was next. Haven said a little prayer before moving the shower curtain out of the way, but still there was no one. She was ready to believe that maybe her senses were just off when she heard a loud thunk come from behind her. Actually, what it sounded like was someone tripping over the trunk at the end of her bed, something she had done on numerous occasions. That's when every cell in her body was telling her to get out of there, to get down to the corner shop and call the police. This was a dangerous situation, and she wasn't prepared for it. She didn't want to be just another news story about a woman who ran towards the danger instead of running for help.

Deciding to listen to, finally, listen to her inner voice she quietly started walking towards the front door that stood open. The problem there was that she would have to walk by the bedroom door in order to get out. What if the person was still in there? Or worse, what if they left the bedroom the moment they made the noise, and now they were hiding somewhere else in the apartment? It was only with great effort that the nerves in her stomach didn't vomit out of her mouth, as Haven gritted her teeth together with pure determination.

Taking a deep breath Haven scolded herself for getting lost in the moment, losing precious time while she stood there, over thinking everything. It was a straight shot from where she was to the front door, if she pushed off as hard as she could on the wall she was leaning against she should be able to get a decent amount of speed going before the intruder even knew she was trying to escape.

No more overthinking it, time to move. With that Haven pushed off against the wall and bolted to the front door. Time seemed to move differently during stressful situations, and a normal ten second sprint seemed to take minutes. Right when she was at the door she tried scooping her purse up as she ran by, but she missed it. Instinct had her turn around to grab at it, and that's when the hand shot out of the darkness and grasped her by the arm. Using the momentum that same hand swung her around until she was once again inside the apartment, up against a wall. That hand had a buddy that came up to clamp down on her mouth, and that buddy had a pair of feet that kicked the door closed.

Held up against a wall, with the unknown stranger pushing his body into her own, her mouth covered and her breathing getting shallower with every shaky breath she took, Haven knew she had messed up. She tried pushing the body off of her, but it was like pushing against a brick wall, there was no give to it.

"Don't move. Don't make a sound. You make a sound and you die, got it?" Haven nodded her head as best she could, and the hand came away from her face. She heard the stranger feel around the wall seconds before he found the switch. With the light illuminating the shape in front of her Haven found herself becoming, not only more afraid, but also very pissed off.

"You remember me, don't you, Haven?" James smirked at her. Standing in front of her was the very being she was avoiding by calling in sick earlier in the day. He stared her down, waiting for an answer.

"Yes." Haven's mouth became increasingly dry as she tried to swallow, to bring any moisture into her throat.

"You spilt your tea all over me the other day." His face was so close to hers that she could smell the whiskey on his breath and the cologne on his neck. His anger was evident in his eyes, but Haven didn't understand where his rage was coming from. He was the one that broke into her apartment, not the other way around.

"And you thought a little breaking and entering might even the field?" Her voice squeaked without her permission. He shook her arms, pressing into them tightly with his hands.

"Don't be a smart ass. That's not why I'm here." While he smirked at the squeak James became impatient in an instant and growled at her. Growled. At. Her. It came deep from within his chest and she felt it down to her toes. She needed to get out of here, or he was going to hurt her.

"Then why are you here? In my apartment? Without my permission? Late at night?" The more she thought about the situation, the more trouble she knew that she was in. She lived alone, it was late at night, and no one was expecting to hear from her until the morning. James was known for his rage and his irrational behaviors, and now he was in her apartment and had her up against a wall. He obviously was stronger than her, there wouldn't be much she could do if things took a violent turn.

"You've been keeping busy in your spare time, haven't you?" For a moment Haven thought this was about her taking a sick day, but how would he know what she did with her day away from work?

"How would you know what I've been doing in my spare time?" If James thought keeping her in the dark about what he really wanted was going to get him answers, he was an idiot. She would need a few more pieces of the puzzle before she would have anything of value to say to him.

"Seems you've really been spending a lot of time down at the psych hospital. What's the matter, getting checked out?" His hot breath fanned across her face and down her neck. Haven's nerves were in her throat as she fought to keep herself from vomiting all over him.

"I've been visiting my grandmother, if you must know." She answered him through gritted teeth, trying to keep her breathing even despite the absolute panic that was going on in her head. Why would James care about her family? The entire situation was so unreal that Haven wasn't sure if she was in a dream again. It was getting increasingly hard to breathe and the closeness of his body was starting to make her claustrophobic. Her head started spinning and it was becoming more challenging to focus on what he was saying.

"Tsk, tsk, tsk. We both know that's not the only person you've been visiting, now is it?" Haven stared into his eyes, letting him know that she finally understood why he was here. That one question cleared so much up. He didn't care about her or her grandmother, he was fishing for information about Nova.

"I don't know what you're talking about." Was he talking about Nova? How would he have even known about her, unless he was spying on her somehow. But that line of thought just brought more questions, like why would James care if Haven was visiting Nova? James didn't appear to be the "helping the innocent" type, so did that mean he wanted to hurt Nova? The instinct to protect Nova became stronger, and her immediate reaction was to lie to James. Maybe he didn't know as much as he let on. Even if he knew more, Haven wouldn't be able to live with herself if she gave anything away about Nova, especially to this psychopath.

"Don't lie to me! You've been visiting a Jane Doe." James pulled her away from the wall only to slam her back into it, knocking the air out of her momentarily. Seeing how serious he was Haven was ready to turn the tables on him, hoping to shock him enough to back him up a step or two.

"Yea, I visited her, so what? What's it to you how I spend my time when I'm not at work?" There was no use lying anymore, he obviously knew she wasn't at work earlier, it was the only time she had actually talked to Nova.

"I'm very interested in her, and you're going to tell me everything you know about her." James had Haven pinned to the wall in such a way that she couldn't move a hair. His face was dreadfully close to her, and the harshness of his tone left moisture on her face from him being so close. And yet a new feeling rose up in Haven. Defiance. Well, it was new for her. In the moment she didn't have it in her to question where this feeling was coming from, she just knew it was taking over her very tired and very confused body, so she was going to go with it.

"No," Haven said with so much conviction and confidence that she almost impressed herself.

"Excuse me?" James, however, wasn't as impressed. Instead, his rage was flowing off of him in waves. But this was no time to back down.

"I said, no! Now get out before I call the cops!" Her voice was getting louder, and she hoped that one of her neighbours would be home, hear the argument, and call the cops. The fury in James' eyes started to burn into her.

"No one says no to me, now tell me what I want to know!" With that he slammed Haven against the wall a few more times, just enough to really knock the wind out of her. He was a fully-grown adult on the verge of a very violent toddler temper tantrum. Haven knew she needed to find a way to either calm him down or get herself out of there.

"Why are you so interested in Jane Doe?" If she was lucky maybe James would let slip his real motive when it came to Nova. Coughing, Haven fought to keep talking. Her entire back was on fire, and she knew there would be bruising in multiple places.

"That is none of your business!" James was full on raging out, so much so that his body was shaking with every breathe the was taking.

"You expect me to tell you everything I know and yet you won't tell me a thing? Why on earth would I do that?" James pulled Haven in nice and close, to make sure she really understood what was going to happen should she defy him.

"For starters, either you tell me what I want to know, or you'll be out of a job within days. That not enough inspiration for you? Then how about you tell me what I want to know and I won't touch a hair on poor grandma's head?" He was taunting her, and she knew it, yet she couldn't help the way she reacted when he threatened her grandmother. Every nerve on her body started acting out.

"No!" As tears flooded her eyes, Haven kicked out at James, causing him to stumble. Haven saw the book sitting beside her on the floor, where she dropped it when he swung her around, picked it up and started swinging at James' head. He immediately put his arms up to protect his head.

"Leave my grandmother alone!" One final hit and Haven dropped the book, ran back to the door, threw it open and ran out the door, down the stairs, and out onto the street. She could hear James close behind her, so she kept on moving. She didn't know where she was going, she only knew that she couldn't give him the information that he wanted, and she couldn't let him hurt her grandmother.

Haven ran down the street to the closest corner store, turning around every so often to see if she was being followed. At first, she saw James not to far behind her, but the closer to the store she got, the closer the distance between her and James. She ran up to a couple just getting out of their car to ask them to help her, but when she turned around James had disappeared. The couple looked frazzled, and Haven apologized for spooking them. They called the cops for her and waited with her until they showed up.

The cops searched her apartment but there weren't any signs of a break in. The only evidence that something happened were the bruises up and down her arms and on her back that were starting to form.

"Now, tell me again, who do you think was in your apartment?" The officer had asked her this three times already, phrasing it differently as if to catch her in a lie. Frustrated, she took a deep breath before answering yet again.

"I told you; it was James Hunter." The officer gave her another unimpressed look.

"James Hunter? The very same James Hunter that just happens to be one of the top businessmen in our city?" Haven nodded, knowing this wasn't going well.

"He also is sort of my bosses' boss, if you must know. It sounds crazy, but it was him! Shouldn't you be bringing him in for questioning, or something? Isn't that your job?" Haven's patience was wearing thin, and the officer seemed to be having the same issue.

"Ma'am, I'm not going to put an APB out on one of the most well-known men in our city. Not that I don't believe you, it's just I'm having a hard time figuring out what someone with the kind of money he has would be doing breaking into your small, one-bedroom apartment." Haven couldn't believe it. James was going to get away with threatening her and her grandmother. If he was still out there that meant Nova wasn't safe, either.

"So, you're saying that you're going to do nothing. Great." The disappointment coated every word that came out of Haven's mouth.

"Not nothing. We'll track James down, discreetly, and ask him where he was tonight. If he has an alibi then my hands are tied. I'm sorry." Haven nodded her head and said goodnight, going back inside her apartment and locking the door.

After everything had settled down and the police had gone Haven sat on her bed, trying to understand what was happening to her. It felt right, putting herself between James and Nova. But what would the cost be? There were no answers to be found in the quiet apartment. Haven turned and looked at the book of stories. There was something that she was missing, some piece of information that would make everything suddenly make sense. Haven walked over and picked the book up, placing it on her bed and curling up next to it.

CHAPTER TWENTY-ONE

James

James had made his way back to his place, keeping one hand on his head where that bitch hit him with the book. There was a ringing in his ears, and he had a cut on his forehead, he would make her pay for that. It had become too risky when she got out to the store, he had to let her go. Damn it! He should have never let her get that far; he just wasn't expecting her to actually fight back.

Silencing her would be slightly complicated because she worked for the company, and if she just disappeared, they could possibly be investigated. Not that they wouldn't be able to handle it, but if the police started sniffing around the company the board would have his head. That being said, if that bitch swung that monstrous book at him one more time, he would have no problem taking her out, company and board be damned.

James was seething. This entire project was supposed to be simple. He had a list of names, and he was supposed to just pick them off one by one, restore his family's honour and finish off what his ancestors had started. As far as the list went, Nova was meant to be one of the easy ones to cross off the list. She was a college kid for fuck sakes with zero real world experience. Once her parents were dead she shouldn't have lasted more than twenty-four hours. But one hiccup here, and one pesky police patrol car there, and she managed to slip out from under him. Add one pain in the ass employee to medal in the mix and this project was starting to unravel.

If only he could get his hands on Nova, more specifically her neck, he could close this chapter and move on. He was so close. He could feel it in the air. He could sense her fear. She was the hardest one to find so far, it had taken his company over six months to pin down her location to this city, surprisingly the same city that was the centre location of his family's company. They had spent years building up their public image and client base, years to make it seem like they were an honorable, presentable company. All of that so he could undergo a massive project behind the scenes without anyone sniffing around and asking questions. The project had been going on for the past two years now, and there were a few successes, not enough in his opinion though. There had also been a few bumps in the road, which is why it took so long to track her down.

If James had thought Nova had done any of it on purpose, hiding right under their noses and getting herself detained in an institution, he would have had respect for her. To pull that off, on purpose, at her age, would have shown an understanding of what or who was hunting her and the danger she was actually in. However, he was sure she just got lucky one to many times, and that pissed him off. It made him look bad to the investors, not to mention his father. Not lucky enough though. He still found her. She was being held in the psychiatric hospital. Some cop brought her in after she was found ranting and raving about the wolves coming to get her. Everyone thought she had snapped, but James knew she was right. He was coming to get her, and he was going to end her.

He was on a time-crunch though. Word would be getting out soon about his lack of success and his father would be on the phone, ripping into him for the mess he was making of this entire situation. James was sure if he could get everything settled before that conversation then he would be able to survive the wrath coming his way.

The only thing that stood in his way at the moment was the seventy-two-hour solitary hold that Nova had been placed on. There was no way for him to sneak in without alerting the security team. They hadn't had time to secure a person on the inside yet, but give it another couple of days and James would be able to walk right in and take care of business. That's alright, for now he knew where she was, and he felt confident biding his time. In seventy-two hours she would be dead.

She was alone, not a friend in the world, not one person that believed her. What could happen in seventy-two hours while she was under a hold that could undermine his plan now? He just had to sit back and be patient. It was like shooting fish in a barrel.

James poured himself a glass of bourbon and stared at himself in the mirror while he drank it in one swallow. One more glance at himself, at the fucking bump growing on the side of his head, and his anger came back ten-fold. James tossed his glass at the mirror, allowing the glass to shatter and fall everywhere. Fucking mail room girl.

CHAPTER TWENTY-TWO

Haven

I t was some time before she could fall asleep, and even then, it wasn't a sound sleep. Haven tossed and turned all night long, dreams about wolves eating innocent people plagued her. Haven started staring at her front door, getting up every so often to check and recheck that everything was locked up, and then laying back down again. After dozing for just under an hour, Haven finally closed her eyes to welcome sleep. A minute later her phone went off. Haven jumped out of her skin, and then reached for it, not even looking to see who was calling.

"Hello?" Haven answered in a raspy sleep voice as she tried to stop the shaking that had taken hold in her hands.

"Hi, sorry to disturb you so late, but I'm calling for a Ms. Haven Conners." The voice on the other side of the phone was solemn. Haven sat straight up in her bed, immediately alert. There was no way that this call was good news, and she knew there was only one reason she would be getting a call like this, and in that instant her heart shattered into pieces.

"That's me." She swallowed hard, waiting for the inevitable news, the news that would destroy her.

"Hi Haven, it's Doris from the Red Ceaders Psychiatric Hospital. I'm so sorry to bother you so late at night, but it's your grandmother. She's taken a turn for the worse. I'm afraid she doesn't have much time left; she's getting weaker by the hour. It might be best if you came in to see her." Before the nurse could even finish that sentence, Haven was out of bed, running through her apartment, and shoving her bare feet into the sneakers by the door.

"I'm on my way!" Haven grabbed her purse automatically as she flew out the door. The run to her car and the drive to the hospital didn't even register to Haven, her only concern was getting to her grandmother. She was trying her best not to fall apart. There would be time for that later. Haven wanted to make sure she was as composed as possible, if only to help her grandmother through this final moment in life as best she could. If all she could do was be a friendly face sitting there as her grandmother passed on then she would be sure to do just that.

The parking lot of the institution was practically empty, Haven was in such a daze that she had to go back to her car twice to get the keys out of the ignition. When she finally made it to the front of the building she took a deep breath and then went for the door.

Normally all of the doors would be locked at this time of night, but one of the night guards was waiting for her and escorted her into the building and straight to her grandmother's room. He didn't say much as they walked together, but the look on his face told her everything she needed to know. Her grandmother didn't magically start getting better. This was really it— this was the end. Turning the corner Haven's first look at her grandmother took all the air out of her lungs.

It had only been a few days since Haven had seen Betty, but her grandmother looked awful. Her face was pale, her cheekbones were protruding. She was propped up but, as Haven got closer, she could hear how hard it was for her grandmother to breathe. Haven ran from the doorway to her side, doing her best to keep the tears at bay.

"Grandma, I'm here now." Haven took her hand, noticing how cold it was. How could she have gone downhill so fast in a couple of days? There were a few nurses in the room but the head nurse, one that Haven knew by sight, ushered everyone out of the room, giving Haven a little privacy to say the hardest goodbye of her life.

"Haven. My sweet Haven." Betty's voice sounded like it was coming from beyond the grave already. Betty attempted to sit up more, but Haven put a hand on her shoulder, telling her without words to stay down. The whites of Betty's eyes were bloodshot and tinged yellow.

"Shhh...save your strength." Betty relaxed back into her bed and attempted to clear her throat, but ended up choking on her own saliva. It took a few minutes and a sip or two of water before Betty was stabilized and tried speaking again. Haven couldn't believe this was the woman that had raised her. She had been so strong every time Haven needed her, and now she was barely breathing, lying in a hospital bed, unable to speak properly. This was all that was left of Haven's family, and she was fading away.

"No, this is important. I need to tell you ... there is something I've been keeping from you all these years." The look in Betty's eyes was the only thing that kept Haven from shushing her again. This formidable woman wanted to say something before her time on this earth was over, who was Haven to deny her that. As she started talking, it was difficult for Haven to understand Betty's speech as she was starting to slur her words. Looking around, Haven noticed the doctor wasn't even around. It was mostly the nightly nursing staff and a few security guards that had gathered around the nurses' station outside of the room. Even then, it was mostly staff that had been there since the start of Betty's stay. She had become a well-loved member of the institution, and the staff were gathering to pay their respects. While she was honored at the show of support, Haven wanted nothing more than to shout at them all, to tell them that Betty wasn't gone yet. Haven wanted to tell them to get out of her sight, Betty didn't need to see all of their sad eyes. That wasn't the last thing she should see on this Earth.

Haven tried focusing back on Betty, who was still trying to choke out her message for her granddaughter.

"Haven, you must listen to me. This is important. This is about where you come from. You're a very special soul. You come from a very special bloodline." Betty was trying to hold Haven's attention and all Haven could do was hold her hand and try her hardest to stay in the moment without falling apart. Haven was trying to memorize it all. The way her grandmother talked, the sound of her voice, the way she always smelled of peppermint. Betty was never one to be ignored though, and she pulled Haven back into the conversation with a shake of her hand.

"And because of that—" Betty started coughing and gesturing to the water on her side table. Haven lifted it up to her mouth to give her a sip.

"Because of that, oh... the adventures you'll have! But you'll also... also have to face some of your biggest ... nightmares along ... the way." Every word was coming out slower than the last, her breathing becoming more and more strained, and Haven wasn't ready for it. The glint in Betty's eyes was starting to fade, her voice was becoming weaker every sentence that she uttered. The hold Haven had on her own emotions was starting to slip as a single tear started rolling down her face. The emotion of it all was becoming too much to hide inside. Haven cleared her throat and tried talking.

"Grandma, what are you talking about? You aren't making much sense." What was it with the nightmare talk? The wheels in Haven's brain started turning. Talking about nightmares wasn't something Betty ever did. Did her grandmother know something about the dreams she had been having about the girl and the wolf? Should Haven even be worrying about it in this moment? Shouldn't she be trying to focus on saying goodbye to her grandmother? And yet, a small part of her brain couldn't let the curiosity go. Thankfully her grandmother didn't make her wait long for an answer. Talking as if Haven knew what she was referring to, Betty kept going.

"Your big adve-nture, my dear, the ... one you have ... secretly been missing. The one ... you've been waiting for. It's right here. Right in ...front of your eyes." Betty started coughing again and Haven gave her another few sips of water, a few drops coming out of the side of her mouth.

"I know you ... can't see it yet, but you will. You need to ... help her. The po-or girl that you've ... been worried about, she needs your help. You're the only one th-th-that can do it." Was she talking about Nova? Who else could she be talking about? Betty's voice was becoming softer and grittier as she talked.

"Grams, please, I don't understand what you're saying. It's confusing, and you should be saving your strength!" Haven's hands were starting to sweat, and her heartbeat was speeding up. Haven glanced at the nurses' station and it looked like they were, once again, being given privacy. Betty patted Haven on the back of the hand in a calming gesture. The next words out of Betty's mouth were so quiet that Haven almost had to put her ear right beside Betty's mouth.

"Nothing to be ... worried about. Nothing to b-b-be scared of. You have it in your heart to be b-b-brave, so be brave for me now. That ... girl is being hunted d-d-own, the fates knew that th-this would happen one day, and that's w-w-why you are so ... drawn to her. You're drawn to pr-rotect her." While her grandmother's words were coming out broken and slowly, Haven could feel the determination behind them.

"What?" Haven was certain now that Betty was talking about Nova. What was the connection there? If Betty knew about Nova, did she also know about James? It felt like the entire world was in on a joke that no one bothered to tell Haven about. A dying grandmother and a stranger in trouble.

"It's ... in your b-b-blood. It's because of your ... ancestors, th-they helped her f-family out ... hundreds of years ago." Betty started coughing in a bad way. A nurse even rushed in to check on her. As quickly as Haven was pulled in, she just as quickly pulled back to the very serious reality of her grandmother slipping away right in front of her.

"Grandma." Haven waited until the nurse left, and then tried to figure out how to tell her grandmother that nothing else mattered in this moment. How do you tell someone on their death bed that they are talking crazy and making no sense?

"The Gr-r-rimm Brothers. They were ... your great, great, great uncles! Haven, it's true! I m-m-may have left out a f-few 'greats' but it ... doesn't make it less t-true. And that g-girl comes from a ... different family line. But the stories, the history is ... in the stories." Betty's voice was becoming louder, but squeakier, as if she was running out of air. Haven was trying to calm her down by feeding into her delusion. Part of her, though, part of her wanted to believe it.

"What history? What stories? Grandma, you're getting worked up. We need to calm you down." But Betty was too far gone already. She was no longer calmly focused on Haven. Betty was trying to claw her way out of her bed, almost to get right into Haven's lap.

"Hers! Little R-r-red Riding Hood's! Nova!" Haven was trying to hold Betty back without hurting her. She was on death's door a minute ago, where was this strength coming from? Just as she thought it a nurse ran back in, looking just as confused as Haven felt. The nurse helped restrain

Betty, but it was almost unneeded at that point. Betty's body wilted back into her bed, her eyes glazed over, and the coughing started up again. Haven's head was just swimming. What the hell was going on here? What just happened?

There wasn't much time for an explanation. Moments after Betty uttered Nova's name her pulse started weakening. Haven couldn't breathe as the nurse came up and squeezed her shoulder, as a show of support, but to let her know that this was it.

The only family she had left was slipping away on her, right in front of her eyes, and there wasn't anything she could do about it. The tears started flowing undeterred. Haven held Betty's hand and uttered soothing words to her, momentarily forgetting what Betty had told her. The nurse backed away once Betty had calmed down, waiting for the inevitable, and letting Haven say goodbye.

There wasn't much that Haven could think to say, so instead she went with her gut.

"Once upon a time, in a small cottage at the edge of the forest, lived a young girl. Everyone called her Little Red Riding Hood ..." It had been Betty's favorite story over the years and Haven wanted it to be the last thing Betty heard.

An hour later Betty was dead. Her body lied there on the bed while Haven sobbed and grieved. Due to it being the middle of the night the nurse was able to give her a little longer to say goodbye.

When it was time, the nurse ushered Haven into a small room just down the hall while the doctor and nurses did their final tests, putting Betty's body to rest underneath a white sheet. Haven rocked back and forth and let the tears come. She didn't care who heard her. She didn't care if she was waking anyone up. The most important, most influential person in her life was now gone. It was almost more than her heart could bear.

After awhile Haven realized she couldn't just sit here. If she was going to have an utter breakdown, she wanted to be in her own home. Her body, however, wasn't as strong as she thought, and she only made it to the bench outside before she had to sit down again and take a few deep breaths. Her body felt numb, she didn't know how to exist in a world that Betty wasn't a part of.

The words Betty spoke started to swirl around her head as she tried to make sense of them. Part of her believed that it was Betty's disease that put these ideas in her head. There was no way she was related to the Grimm Brothers— that would be impossible and more than slightly ridiculous. Haven wasn't the type to be anyone's hero, let alone some scared young girl. Scared, young Nova.

Nova. The poor thing. If Haven felt all alone in the world, how was Nova feeling, locked away and being told that what she feared most of all was a figment of her imagination. Then there was the question of James, why was he so intent of finding out about Nova? Was there some master plot afoot to kill her? None of it made any sense, and yet a small part of her told Haven that the only thing standing between James and defenseless Nova was herself. The question then became how far would she go fulfill her dying Grandmother's last wish? What would she do in order to keep Nova safe— if she could even keep her safe?

Haven got up, made it to her car, and somehow drove home, tears constantly streaming down her face. When she got to her apartment she went straight to her bed and threw herself down. She didn't take her jacket off, she didn't take her shoes off, she barely let go of her purse and locked her door. It had been a hell of a night, and she wouldn't be going to work once again. Her brain was depleted, even James and his break and enter situation was so far from her mind. Haven was numb from the inside out. Taking a deep breath, Haven let the barriers in her mind and heart crumble as she let out a depressing scream, letting the tears come back. Haven cried herself to sleep in that moment. Once asleep her mind brought forth a memory, this time of her own making.

Standing in the kitchen as a young girl with her mother, Haven was packing up a bag of canned goods. Her mother was wearing a well used pair of jeans and a plain flannel shirt. It was almost real enough for Haven to smell the sweet perfume her mom used to wear.

Haven's mother made it a mission to clean out their cupboards every few months with older groceries that could be donated. When she asked her mom why she did this Haven always got the same answer.

"Not everyone is as lucky as we are in this world, Haven. There are people out there that are having a rough time. We are fortunate enough to have food in our fridge, a roof over our head, and warm clothes to wear when we need to. What we should be doing is helping those that don't have that. Just think, if the situation was reversed, wouldn't you want someone to give you a hand? Wouldn't you want someone to offer you the security of knowing where your next meal was coming from?" Her mother's soft voice floated around her, comforting an ache Haven couldn't describe.

Haven went from standing right beside her mother, listening to her voice, to standing right beside Nova's hospital bed. She could still hear her mother's words, words that never came out of her mouth, but looked to direct her. Nova looked even worse than when Haven met her. She was rocking back and forth in her hospital bed, looking around as if she expected someone to appear out of the shadows and attack her. Haven wanted nothing more than to give her a hug and tell her she wasn't alone. Even after everything that had happened that night Haven couldn't help but push her own pain aside at the mere sight of Nova.

"Haven, there are dark forces in this world. Evil that can taint the mind and the heart of anyone. It will sweep across this planet and consume everything it touches. It is made to corrupt and destroy even the purest of hearts, and it will. Unless someone stands in the way. Unless someone makes it stop." As her mother continued to talk a shadow formed in the room. It started off small but then it started creeping its way across the floor and closer to Nova's bed. Nova looked up from the bed into Haven's eyes.

"He's coming for me. Please help." Her voice cracked and the tears came flowing from her eyes. Haven couldn't move from her spot on the floor. Her mother still talking to her.

"Only the most courageous of us will even attempt to stand against it. Be the one to stand against it, Haven. Be the pure heart full of love that the world needs. That Nova needs. It can be terrifying, being the force that stands between evil and its victims. But look in your heart, and know, you are strong enough to win. We don't look the other way, Haven. We don't ignore the people that need our help. It's in our blood to help." Haven turned around and saw her grandmother standing behind her, looking younger and healthier. Glancing back at Nova she saw James forming out of the shadow, his hands turning into claws, striking at Nova.

"Know that we will be with you every step of the way. Believing in you. It's in your blood, Haven. Make it stop, for Nova. Go. Now." With that Haven sat straight up in her bed. The sun seemed to be setting, letting her know that she slept the entire day. Picking up her cell phone she saw that work had tried to call her numerous times, as had the cop she had talked to last night. Everything was spinning out of control, but from that moment on she knew one thing for certain. She needed to get to Nova, tonight.

CHAPTER TWENTY-THREE

Haven

Sitting on the edge of her bed, Haven was trying to come up with a reason to be back at the institution. As frustration set in— frustration in herself for not being someone that could come up with a good plan in a moment's notice— her phone rang.

"Hello?"

"Hi, is this Haven?" a sweet voice on the other end asked.

"Yes, it is."

"Hi, yes, this is nurse Sanderson calling from Red Ceaders. I'm so sorry to disturb you, but there are a few more forms that we need you to fill out. If you would like I could email them to you?" Haven stood up and started to pace.

"No, I can come in to do it. I can come right away, if that's alright?" Trying not to sound too eager wasn't easy. She could have reached into the phone and kissed the nurse for giving her exactly what she needed to go back to Red Ceaders.

"Of course, we'll see you then." The nurse hung up. Haven got up and started heading out of her apartment, grabbing her jacket and purse by the front door.

If luck was on her side the nurse that let her visit Nova the first time would be on shift and hopefully let Haven in the room. After that it was up to her to come up with a way to get Nova out, past all of the security checks. Haven stopped for a second before locking her door and thought about it. This was crazy. Breaking someone out of an institution was dangerous, and probably illegal. What was she even doing?

Closing her eyes and resting her head on the door to her apartment, Haven took a breath. Immediately the image of Nova being chased by the wolf, and the terror in her eyes flashed into Haven's head. It could all go wrong, it could fall apart, and she could end up in jail, but if she didn't at least try she would never forgive herself. Haven opened her eyes, locked the door, and started hurrying down the hallway, mentally trying to work out how she was going to convince Nova to come with her.

There were so many moving pieces to the puzzle, answers that she didn't have, and yet she kept putting one foot in front of the other. She would find a way, somehow. Failure simply wasn't an option at this point. Betty's spirit was with her. Her mother's spirit was with her. Haven hoped that would be enough.

When she got to the institution Haven was bombarded with condolences from all of the staff, as they knew her and her grandmother well. The nurse that called her had met her in the waiting room and brought her to one of the nurses' stations to finish signing the forms. Haven filled out what she needed to while trying to casually look around for the nurse from the day before. Her heart was beating in her chest so hard that Haven thought everyone around her could hear it. Trying to look calm and collected, the dutiful granddaughter there to collect a few personal items while she was grieving, Haven kept waiting for someone to call her on it her ulterior motives, but it never happened. As she finished up her signatures the nurse she was looking for walked by and stopped to offer her condolences.

"Betty was one of my more memorable clients. She never liked to cause trouble, but she did like to learn about our family lives. Working here can be tough at times and Betty was always a bright spot on rough days." Haven loved hearing things like that about Betty. Even as her disease took her memories Betty still cared about the people around her. This was the perfect segue and it left Haven wondering about the forces of the universe.

"I know what you mean. The last time I had a good conversation with her she mentioned Nova, and how worried she was about her. With Nova being so young and not having family, Betty was worried about her." Crossing her fingers and toes that the nurse would take the bait, Haven waited.

"I'll be honest, I don't know if it's wishful thinking, but since you popped in there to say hi to her there has been a small bit of progress. She actually ate a few bites here and there today. I almost think I can see the hint of color coming back to her face. Now, it's nothing huge, but every step is a step towards recovery, right?" Haven nodded along, hoping this would mean the nurse would let her back in again.

"Really? That's amazing! That's something that I would like to see, do you think that would be possible while I'm here?" Haven held her breath as the nurse looked around for a moment.

"Well, I mean, it did seem to do something for her last time. We really should get clearance, so we don't have to break the rules to do this. There will be some paperwork to fill out and then it needs to be approved." Haven took a deep breath, looked around and noticed no one else was around them. It was now or never.

"I don't really have time to fill out any forms at the moment, but I can always come back another day to make this official. I'd like to keep visiting her if I can, to see if I can help. Until then, though, I would like to just say hi quickly right now, if I can." Haven could see the nurse not fully appreciating the request, but Haven kept pushing.

"I just would feel so much better knowing that I checked on her. I know she doesn't have family checking in on her, and it's something Betty would have wanted me to do. You said it helped her last time, maybe after a quick visit she'll have an even better day tomorrow! But only if it's not much trouble." Haven waited a mere couple of seconds before the nurse caved.

"Alright, in honour of Betty, but it's the last time I can sneak you in there Haven, you know I could lose my job for this." Nodding along with the nurse Haven gave her what she hoped was an encouraging smile.

"I understand one hundred percent. I'll be quick and no one will ever know I was in there." As the words came out of her mouth, guilt flooded her system, knowing that what she had planned was going to cause some trouble. To put it simply, she had no other choice. Haven followed the nurse down the hallway, sweat coating the inside of her palms as her heart thudded against her chest uncontrollably.

There was a security stop just down the hall from the room that Nova was in, and Haven couldn't help but wonder if the security guard could tell what her intentions were just by looking at her. Having him so close to Nova's room would make busting her out even more precarious. It made Haven question her own intentions yet again. Was it worth it to put herself out there like this, worth putting the nurse's job in danger? Would the consequences be more than she could handle? No one really knew what she was doing here, it would be easy to turn around and never think of these crazy stories again.

However, the moment she snuck into the room that rationalization flew out the window. Nova looked rough. She obviously hadn't been eating or sleeping much in the past couple of days. Her hair looked stringy, her skin had the colour of ash, and her lips were dry and cracked. The dark circles that surrounded her eyes emphasized how sunken her eyes really looked. If the nurse thought that this was a slight improvement, she may have been looking through rose-colored glasses. The worst part of it all was how dead inside Nova looked. Those eyes were hollow, almost no life behind them. Haven could feel it in her gut, Nova was dying in here. Even if James never came, Nova was so far gone and had been so traumatized that there was almost no hope for her now. Haven was her last shot.

"Hi Nova, do you remember me?" Haven stood in the doorway with a nurse, waiting to be acknowledged by Nova. With a slight nod of Nova's head, the nurse left the two girls alone, mouthing five minutes to Haven. Nodding her understanding, Haven walked all the way into the room. Once the door was closed Haven ran to Nova's side.

"We don't have a lot of time, but you need to get up. I'm getting you out of here, tonight." Haven tried to find the words to explain what she was doing, but it all sounded so fake and suspicious, even to herself.

"What?" Nova's voice croaked out. Haven knelt down to look her in the eyes. Nova's soul was withering away, and it was all shown in her eyes. This was a girl so hopeless and defenseless; Haven didn't know how or what brought her into Nova's life, but she was in it now. She was in it, and she'd be damned if she would rest until she made a difference.

"Long story short, the guy that I sort of work for, or at least worked for up until last night, is possibly on his way here to hurt you tonight." Haven found a simple pair of sneakers under the bed, laces of course were taken out of them, but they were better than nothing. She started putting them on Nova, feeling the rush and apprehension of not knowing how long they had before someone would be coming through the door.

"You're starting to sound as crazy as me." Nova felt like her limbs were full of rocks, everything felt heavy and made it harder to move. How long had she been in here and what was this woman doing? Was this a trick? Was this Haven here to lure her out for the wolf to take her somewhere he could get to her?

"It may be crazy but it's also true. He attacked me in my apartment last night and kept asking me about you." Haven was aware how suspicious this sounded, but she had very little time to persuade Nova into believing her. After a moment in silence, Nova was still a little weary, so Haven pulled out her cell phone and used it to bring up James' work profile which had a current photo of him on her company's website. Haven held the phone up in front of Nova.

"This is the man that threatened me last night. Does he look familiar to you?" Nova came alive when she saw the picture, backing up as if it would bite her, and ultimately falling off of the bed in shock. Her breathing started coming faster and faster and her eyes became so wide, it was almost comedic. She started pointing at Haven's phone, her arm shaking as she did it.

"That's the guy in my dreams, the guy that turns into the wolf!" Nova's voice shook with every word and Haven could feel the fear coming off her. Nova stood up and backed herself into a corner in the room, shaking her head back and forth, scrunching her eyes closed. Haven could see the disbelief on her face.

"And he's the guy that's headed here, tonight, to see you. We have to get you out of here." Nova's eyes snapped open as she looked over at Haven with distrust in her eyes. Haven's words from a few moments earlier started to come back to her.

"You work for him? You just said you work for him. Are you here to bring me to him? Please, I didn't do anything, please don't help him!" Haven was taken aback, but by putting herself in Nova's shoes she could see where the misunderstanding was coming from. A panic attack was brewing inside of Nova and Haven had mere moments to find a way to disarm it so they could move forward. Haven held an arm out, like someone would try to calm an upset child or animal. Haven spoke quickly but calmly, trying to keep any panic out of her voice.

"Nova, I know that there is no possible way for me to one hundred percent convince you right now that I am on your side, not his. We don't have time for that, but please believe me enough to come with me." Haven and Nova made direct eye contact and Haven could sense that Nova was torn on what was real and what wasn't. Haven hoped that she came across as genuine. There would be no way to save Nova if Nova refused to trust her. Waiting for a moment to see what Nova would decide, Haven was relieved when Nova gave her a nod of understanding.

"Okay. But how are we supposed to get out of here? They aren't just going to let me walk out the front door. And there is a security guard stationed right outside." Haven opened her purse and started pulling an extra pair of sweatpants, and sweater out of her bag. She had found them in her car and shoved them into her purse, just in case. It was a miracle that security didn't see these items as a risk.

"Quickly, put these on." Haven was flying by the seat of her pants, hoping that everything would work out. While Nova forced her tired and sore body into the oversized clothing, Haven was peeking out the window in the door down the hallway, towards the security station. The best option that they had was to wait for him to look away or to go walk his rounds.

While she was spying on the security guard, he seemed to get a call on his radio. He spoke for a moment, looked right at Nova's room, and then started walking away from his desk. That was odd, thought Haven. He was the only security guard on duty in this wing. If he wasn't there, and it didn't appear as if a replacement was showing up, what would stop someone from just walking out?

That's when it hit Haven. If no one was outside the room anyone could leave, but also anyone could walk in without worry. The air in Nova's room started to get thicker, making it harder for Haven to swallow, and her breathes were starting to come in slow, shallow breathes. They had to get out, now.

"Nova, we must go, now! James is close!" Haven picked up her bag and took Nova's appearance in. She looked a little raggedy, the clothing was a bit big on her, but that may work in their favour. Nova stumbled to the door; disbelief written all over her face.

They opened the door, slowly at first, not sure if someone would be coming around the corner. All the nurses seemed to be occupied some-where else. There was an emergency exit down the hallway and around the corner, Nova had noticed it one day, but never thought she would be one that got to use it.

"Why aren't we moving?" asked Nova.

"Just trying to figure out which hallway is our best choice." Haven was almost paralyzed, knowing that if she chose wrong, they would never get out safely. Deciding that taking a chance and choosing was better than standing still and getting caught, Haven she grabbed Nova's hand and dragged her to that hallway. There were a few patients in the halls, but no one really took notice of the two women. The nurses at the station were busy filling out paperwork, meaning no one had eyes on Nova's room or the two women sneaking down the hall.

The real worry came when it was time to go around the corner. Haven poked her head around it and saw that the coast was clear. Not wanting to draw attention to them they casually walked to that door. Just as they got to it there was a loud crash in the room that use to hold Nova. The loud noise started to garner attention from everyone in the hall, the nurses included. Both girls looked at each other, knowing someone was on their trail, but also knowing that it would become very clear in mere moments that they were missing, they needed to get out now. Haven pulled Nova through the emergency exit, into the night, down the stairs, around the building, and to her car in the parking lot.

Haven's hands shook fiercely as she tried to get the key in the ignition, but on the third try she jammed it in there, turned the key, and before she could give it another thought, Haven peeled out of the parking lot, officially having broken Nova out of the institution.

CHAPTER TWENTY-FOUR

James

When it came down to either putting one of their own men on the inside or paying off the guard that already worked there, paying off the guard turned out to be rather easy. Times were tough and loyal employees were hard to find in this economy.

After relaying to the guard what he needed James was informed that he would have a twenty-minute window to get this job done, more than enough time in his opinion. Nova was in an isolated room without anything to defend herself. She wouldn't even have shoes on. Once he tied up this loose end he could move on to the rest of the project.

Once the sun finally went down and his people confirmed that the coast was clear, James was ready to make his move. His team had ensured that any armed doors were deactivated and any cameras pointing his way were functioning on a time loop, giving him multiple different access points to the building. He had a map of the first floor already memorized so he would know right where to go. Any hesitations would slow him down and he planned on being miles away when her body was discovered.

James entered the building without issue, keeping his pace fast enough, but not to fast as to breed suspicion. The security guard was standing at the front desk, talking to the nurse there. When he saw James, he angled himself in a way that had the nurse's back to the waiting room. James walked lightly on his feet and slipped through the security door. Winding his way through the halls James kept running over his plan in his mind. Turning the last corner James walked right up to the door, took a quick second to glance down the hallway, ensuring that there were no witnesses, and he let himself into the room. He stepped inside. It was dark, but it only took a quick second for him to realize that he was the only one in there. The bed was empty and there was no where else for her to hide in that room. Rage built up in his veins as his plans seemingly, once again, went sideways. Unable to control himself, James made quick work of ripping the bed from the floor and tossing it around the small room, making sure he wasn't missing anything. The metal of the frame clanged and with the emptiness of the room, the noise echoed off of the four walls. The unencumbered rage that was flowing through him rose so quickly that it left James violently shaking in anger.

This wasn't supposed to be how things went, he had a plan! To his left he spotted a metal tray with some food on it sitting on the table. Touching the bottom of the tray he realized it was still warm. She had to still be close. If a nurse had delivered her dinner she couldn't be to far away. Instantly he knew, fucking Haven had something to do with this. She was becoming a pain in his ass; he was going to strangle the life out of her. James stormed out of the room and started looking down the different hallways. Gone was his calm composure, and in its place was the feral snarl of a wild animal. Instantly he pressed a small button on the earpiece he was wearing, allowing him to communicate with his team.

"She isn't fucking here but she can't be far. Find her!" His tech team started pouring over the video footage, looking for any sign of Nova while James started pacing the hallways, every step he took only encouraged the rage to take over his body. Clenching his fists together James waited for answers. It took mere seconds before his team got back to him, they had found her. That's why they were his employees, he accepted nothing less that perfection as an employer.

"Found her. Looks like she went out the west side emergency exit. She wasn't alone either." He fucking knew it. He would bet every cent to his name that fucking Haven Conners was behind the jail break.

James was out of control, he had to rein it in and focus. There was time to rage out later, like when he had Nova's pretty little neck under his hands. The west side door, that was one of the doors with an alarm on it, unfortunately thanks to his team no one would have noticed it being open with all the alarms being shut off. For someone that was supposed to be an easy kill weeks ago, this bitch was grating more and more on his nerves.

The next time he saw either of these women he was going to pull the nails from their fingers, slowly, before taking them out for good. James punched one last wall before letting himself out the nearest exit. With the commotion that he made nurses were starting to investigate what was going on. They would check on Nova's room, find her missing, and the cops would be called. James was determined to be long gone before then.

"Find them! Now!" he barked his orders out to his team once he hit the parking lot. While they were searching for evidence of the now two missing girls, James started to head over to Haven's place. There weren't many places they could hide from him and his people. Haven wasn't an idiot, she would want to get out of town, but a girl who stayed in one place for a family member had a sentimental side. She would want to grab a few items from her apartment. That would be her final and fatal mistake.

CHAPTER TWENTY-FIVE

Haven

The air in the car was heavy, both women were trying their best to keep their breathing controlled. Nova's head was on a swivel, keeping an eye on every direction, looking for danger.

"We must be quick. He's been to my house; he knows where I live." Going against her own gut, Haven drove straight to her apartment, hoping to grab a few items before getting Nova out of the city. A move she would have shamed any character for in a horror movie. If she would have been more prepared, they could have left immediately, but as it was, she was merely going moment to moment, and she needed to be sure there was nothing of importance for her to go back for later on. She knew her apartment wasn't safe, James already showed her that. There was no where else in the city that she knew of where they could hide. Logically, they had to leave, they had to get out, and fast.

The streets appeared emptier than normal and the silence between the two girls in the car stretched out what should have been a quick car ride, or at least that was how it felt. Both women internally going over everything that just happened. Haven had gotten Nova out of there just in the nick of time, barely. A few minutes longer and they both knew Nova would have never seen the light of day again.

Haven steadied her breathing, doing her best to keep a clear head and to not panic. Up until the last hour or so all her concerns felt somewhat made up. Almost as if she were creating a story in her own head. But knowing someone had actually come to find Nova, to hurt her, confirmed everything Haven felt inside about it. Nova needed help, and there was literally no one around to help her, except for Haven.

Haven couldn't let any other thoughts of what if cloud her mind. She had to keep thinking one or two steps ahead, especially if she wanted to get out of the city unharmed. Looking over at Nova, Haven could see the thoughts flying around in her mind.

"Nova?" It took a minute for Nova to respond.

"I just...I can't believe any of this. It almost doesn't even feel real. Is this a dream? A nightmare? Someone is hunting me. I'm sure of it...almost. But all these professionals were trying to tell me it was all in my head, that none of it was real. I started to question my own sanity. They almost had me believing that I had really lost my mind." Nova looked over at Haven.

"But you make me feel seen. You aren't making fun of me. You see the threat, too. And that makes me feel a little bit less alone." Haven lifted the corner of her mouth in a small smile, but then Nova kept talking.

"As appreciative as I am for that, I just can't see the good through all the bad here. Someone hurt my parent's. Killed them. Now they want to hurt me, and all I do is keep running. I ran from the institution. I ran from the police back in my hometown. All I do is run. I am just so...tired. I'm exhausted from running. I know you won't have a solution. There is no easy way to fix any of this. I just...had to say some of it out loud." With that Nova looked away and out the window of the car. Not knowing how to respond, Haven focused on driving.

When they reached the apartment Haven told Nova to stay where she was, to keep the doors locked and to stay out of sight. Haven ran into her apartment, taking the stairs faster than she ever had before, and rushing into her place. She threw a bag of items together, including any cash she had in the apartment, a few extra pieces of clothing, and, of course, the story book from her grandmother. Picking up the book felt odd, almost as if the book itself was humming with energy.

Nothing felt real, her apartment didn't even seem like her apartment anymore. Knowing how easy it was for James to break in and attack her made running from the apartment even more satisfying. Taking one last look around at the place, at the safe home she had created for herself, and the life that she was throwing away, and shed a tear. That was all she would allow herself, however, was one. Only one, at least until she got Nova somewhere safe. Haven closed the door, locked it, and headed back to her car, all the while trying to figure out how to save a young girls life.

When she got back to the car Haven changed the plan and, instead of getting into the driver's seat, Haven ran over to the passenger's side and opened the door. Nova's face looked startled at the abrupt change. Haven started speaking quickly, but quietly.

"Come one, we can't take the car. We must leave it here." Nova stared at her like she was the one that just broke out of the institution, but before she could say anything, Haven explained her thinking.

"The company has my license plate on file for parking purposes. I don't want to take any chances that James can track us. If he found you as a Jane Doe at the institution then we need to assume he is everywhere, all the time. We have to start running on foot." Haven pulled Nova out of the car.

"Running on foot, again. How did I not see this coming?" Haven smirked at the sarcasm coming out of Nova's mouth.

"Are you sure leaving the vehicle behind isn't a mistake?" Nova took one last longing look at the car.

"We could chance it, but I doubt luck will be on our side. It'll be easier to disappear in a crowd this way. I hope." Haven grabbed Nova's hand, looked around the neighborhood, and started leading Nova away from the parking lot and into the unknown.

Both girls started speed walking down the sidewalks, ducking through alleys, on their way to some unknown location. Nova hoped Haven had some idea of where they should be going, at least what direction would be best to get out of town. The two girls stayed as quiet as they could, no excess talking to draw attention to them. Every time they saw a car drive past, they ducked behind dumpsters or trees. The night air had produced goose bumps on their skin, or was it the anticipation of the unknown, either way the chill made its way down their spines.

Haven hadn't let go of Nova's hand, not once, either because it was easier to lead her that way, or because Haven could tell that Nova needed that constant reassurance and support. Nova didn't know which one it was, but she was grateful for the warmth of her hand all the same.

The first stop they made was to an ATM not far from Haven's apartment. She made the snap decision to take out as much money as it would let her. Anything valuable of Nova's was taken away when she was admitted, and since she broke out, she had to leave everything behind. Her wallet, any money she had left, and any personal items that she had with her. Very literally she was a woman with no one and nothing.

Haven could sense the unease in Nova. Giving up control in any type of high stress situation wasn't easy, but Haven believed in her heart that the only way for both of them to make it out of the city and to someplace safe, they would have to stick together. Stick together and keep moving, no matter how broken they both felt on was the inside.

Haven took the wad of money from the machine, trying not to make eye contact with anything that might be a camera, and shoved it in her bag. They wouldn't be able to take out anything from her account once they left town or James would know where they were. Haven had learned that much from all the television shows she watched. Did James have that power? Haven had no idea, but the new mantra running through her head was that 'James was everywhere and knew everything' and it was the only thing that was going to keep them safe. Being overly cautious hopefully would save their lives. Haven grabbed Nova's hand and started pulling her down the street again.

Nova had been mostly quiet ever since they had left the institution, aside from what she said in the car, but Haven didn't want to push her to say much. Nova had to be in shock with everything going on, and truthfully if Nova started asking questions Haven wouldn't have any answers about what they were doing or where they were going, at least not yet. The fact that Nova was following along without any push back showed Haven how desperately broken she was. There was no resistance, and it wasn't blind faith, but it was close enough to it that Haven's heart broke for the state of Nova's soul. They just needed to get somewhere safe and then they could have a good talk, a long talk.

CHAPTER TWENTY-SIX

Nova

The quiet lasted about ten more minutes, before Nova needed to know something, needed at least a small piece of information in order to keep her body moving.

"Where are we going?" Nova's breathing was coming out rough, they had been running steadily and she wasn't in the best shape after being on the run, and then being stuck at Red Ceaders. If it wasn't for the adrenaline pumping through her veins she would have collapsed awhile ago.

"Well, the best thing for us that I can think of is taking the first bus outta town. We find a way to just keep moving, at least until we figure out a way to keep you safe." Haven kept looking down every street before turning them onto it, her head on a constant swivel at every noise they encountered. Her answer to Nova was void of any real plan. It dawned on Nova that Haven was an innocent in all of this. She was winging it and putting herself in danger. Nova stopped dead in the street and pulled her hand away, causing Haven to turn around. Both girls were breathing hard.

"What's the matter?" Haven kept looking around, hoping they weren't being followed, and only half listening to Nova. They were out in the open, it wasn't safe to be here, but Nova couldn't let this go any further. Her emotions were beginning to overcome her, at possibly the worst time. They were in danger, real danger, and while the thought of having someone to help her through this gave her hope, she couldn't let this angel of a woman get hurt because of her. Nova's voice was small, meek, and utterly broken, but she spoke clearly.

"I can't ask you to do this, come on the run with me." Nova was shaking her head and starting to step away from Haven, and that got Haven's full attention. The doubt and terror were pulsing out of Nova's eyes. The road had already been long for her, and she wasn't in the best condition to be starting out. They couldn't afford to stall, but there was a battle going on inside Nova's head and her heart. She was in need of, not just a protector, not just a partner, this woman was in desperate need of a friend who would have grace and patience with her. Nova knew just by looking at her that Haven could do that, be that for her. But Nova didn't have it in her to let someone else get hurt on her behalf.

"You didn't ask, I volunteered." Haven tried reaching for Nova's hand, but Nova stood her ground and backed away a bit more. Nova was finally finding her words and they came flying out of her mouth.

"No, I'm serious Haven. This is crazy; you can't walk away from your life for a stranger! You'll never be able to come back! It's dangerous, it's so risky! Think about everything you would be giving up! I can't ask you to do that for me. You've helped me get this far, and for that I'll always owe you, but this is where we have to part ways. I'll leave town and then James will leave you alone. You can go back to your life before this mess."

Nova was starting to get hysterical. Her voice was starting to tremble, and her body was starting to shake. She was trying to say the right thing, but her brave facade was starting to fade. Haven put her hand on Nova's arm, steading her but not trying to pull her anywhere.

"Nova, take a breath and listen to me. I put myself in this situation. I chose to jump right in and put myself between you and him. He's not going to leave me alone just because you left the city. Things are never going to go back to normal for me. I work for his company, and now I know he's doing some shady shit. I can't sit by knowing that I worked for a company that could be possibly doing some very harmful things to people. They are doing bad things there; I won't go back. And he knows where I live. He won't believe that I don't know where you are anyways. So, I'm safer with you." Haven spoke in a steady voice, keeping eye contact with Nova. Nova could feel the determination in Haven's words, but it was hard to fully believe a stranger would go through all of this for her. She didn't want to move on without Haven. If she was being completely honest, she was terrified of being left on her own again. Yet could she handle it if anything were to happen to Haven? It would be her own fault, and that was something she just couldn't bear.

"We can try talking to him." Nova was so choked up, she struggled to keep talking. She walked over to the nearest alley and leaned against the grimy alley wall and let her emotions take over. Haven walked over to her and kept talking in a comforting voice.

"Nova?" Haven moved back beside her, taking another look around to make sure no one was sneaking up on them. The alley was eerily quiet. Nova took a breath so deep that she almost choked on it. There was more to this, the words Nova didn't want to say out loud, but the words that Nova needed to say here and now. It took another precious moment, but Nova finally looked up at Haven and spoke from her heart.

"I don't want you to get hurt, but I don't want to be out there on my own again. He's going to get me, he's going to catch me, and then he's going to kill me. I'm so scared!" Nova was on the edge of another breakdown. Tears streamed down her face at the statement. Nova knew she was being hunted; she also knew there was no stopping it. The concern for Haven was real, but the terror Nova felt for her own life was easily four times more powerful. Haven stepped forward and took Nova's hand once again.

"Hey, listen to me. I know you're scared, but I want you to know I'm not going anywhere. I won't let you be in this alone. James will not win. He will not get you. Not while I'm alive. We are in this together, the good and the bad. Now, you have every right to be terrified, but I need you to also be brave for me. I'm scared too, but together we can figure this out. We can outsmart him, we can win." Nova let Haven's words sink in for a second. Nova stared her down, looking into her eyes and saw strength and determination.

"But the key is to keep moving, we have to make it to the bus station before he figures out our plan." Haven had barely finished her sentence before Nova threw her hands around Haven, hugging her with all the life she had left in her. She didn't think she had anyone left in her life that would look out for her like that. Nova wanted so badly to believe that what Haven was saying was true. Everything Nova had been through in the past few weeks influenced her psyche, especially going through it all alone. The world was a darker place than it was just a few months ago. But with someone on her side, maybe there was hope for a future. Nova and Haven let go of each other and Nova wiped the tears and snot off of her face.

"We're close to the subway, and it will take us straight to a bus station that I know of. We'll be surrounded by people, so we need to keep an eye open, but hopefully we'll blend right in. Now, let's get out of here and find somewhere safe to be, alright?" Nova nodded, giving Haven a half smile.

CHAPTER TWENTY-SEVEN

Haven

Both women exited the alley and started, once again, scurrying down the street, sticking to the shadows. They made it to the nearest subway station and made their way down the stairs. A train had just docked and was emptying out, and the women were waiting for their turn to board, looking at all of the faces, hoping they wouldn't see James in the mass, when they heard a shout from behind.

"Hey! Stop those girls!" Twenty feet behind them was James and two of his thugs, trying to make their way through the crowd to Haven and Nova. They were so close, how had that bastard found them? While Haven was looking behind her, Nova started getting swept away in the rush of the crowd. Between being on the run and being in the institution, Nova had lost a lot of weight, and a lot of muscle mass. All it took was for one person to bump into her hard enough to dislodge her from her safe spot beside Haven. After that the swarm of people walking by were unknowingly keeping the two women apart. Haven quickly looked for Nova, but the damage had been done and the distance between the two kept growing.

"Haven! Help!" Things were moving in slow motion now. The flow of traffic was dragging Nova closer to James and his thugs, and further away from safety. Nova's lack of strength was a great disadvantage; she couldn't break the crowd, no matter how many times Haven saw her attempting to. Haven started towards her but couldn't push through the mass of people either. A hockey game must have just let out and the crowd itself was rowdy with a win. No one could hear Nova's cries for help over the chanting and cheering of the crowd. Haven's call and cries for help also went unnoticed. Haven tried jumping in the mass but nothing she tried was working. The Chesire smile on James' face when he realized that Nova was being pushed right to him told Haven everything she needed to know. He wanted to hurt Nova and he was going to get what he wanted.

Slowly Haven could see everything going wrong. James was going to hurt Nova, and there was nothing Haven could do about it. The strangest sense of dread hit her stomach, making her sick with the realization that she was not strong enough to keep Nova safe. That fear and terror on someone else's behalf awoke something within her. Without realizing what exactly was happening Haven started to feel differently. She was so focused on Nova that she didn't notice the changes in her own body. Still struggling to get through the crowd, Haven shouted out.

"No...no!" Something happened in that moment. Haven had never felt more desperate, more hopeless, and more furious in all her life. This young woman was brought into her life for protection, and she was going to fail. If James grabbed hold of her there would be no power on this earth that could save her. Betty had told her that her destiny was to help people, was all that just crap? How could she have failed so quickly? Nova's cries were starting to fade into the crowd, how did no one seem to care about this young woman freaking out? It was almost as if something unnatural was helping James out, some type of other worldly power was blending Nova into the crowd so much that no one heard her cries for help. Not even the people she was pushing against.

A small shard of anger spiked inside of Haven. She would not allow James to do this, to erase Nova without anyone caring. She cared, Haven cared and to hell with James and his lackeys. Haven took a deep breath, steeled herself, and started shouting from deep in her gut.

"Move out of the way people! Move it! Excuse me! Nova, push your way through!" Haven was trying to push and claw her way through the crowd. Nova's face was bobbing up and down as the crowd around her was pushing this way and that. Haven could see it, though, the doubt and fear in Nova's eyes. Nova was seconds away from giving up entirely, her body and soul were already so tired. Haven was out of time.

"I can't! Haven, he's going to get me!" Tears were streaming down the young woman's face, her voice hoarse from screaming. She was throwing her body against the crowd and the only thing it accomplished was widening the space between the two of them.

CHAPTER TWENTY-EIGHT

Jax

The room was tense, dark, and the air was heavy. Tall white candles were laid out in a circular pattern around a giant stone table that stood in the center of the room. There were no windows to let light in and the floor was completely made of dirt. The room itself was in the basement of their hideout, and only used for one very specific reason, to bridge the spiritual gap between two people.

The three men occupying the room were each doing their own thing, but all of them were on high alert. Walker was stationed in front of the only door to the room, a sentry ready to defend his leader. His hand was resting on the hilt of a knife that he kept hooked to his belt on his right side. His job was to make sure that nothing and no one interrupted what was happening here.

Watson was leaning against the farthest wall, a heavy ancient book in his hands as he kept studying the text for any answers it may hold. Only once one looked closer could they see four discreet weapons strapped to his body, two knives, one handgun, and a samurai sword strapped to his back.

Jax was lying on top of the stone table, eyes closed, and arms placed palm up resting beside him. For all intense purposes he looked like he was sleeping, resting even. His breathing was deep and even and it appeared as if the all the muscles in his body were relaxed. To the trained observer, however, it was obvious his brain was working harder than his body. His eyes, while closed, were flitting back and forth. For Walker and Watson, it seemed like he had been unconscious for ages. They had to trust that he knew what he was doing; there was no way to reach him where he was. Both brothers shared a look, wonder how long was to long in this scenario.

No one spoke a word, not even in a casual conversation to help pass the time. The only way that time appeared to have past was through the dripping wax on the candles. Suddenly Walker and Watson both came alert at the same time, as Jax's breathing picked up and his fingertips and the tips of his toes started twitching. The flames on the candles started swaying and growing as a growling seemed to come out of the shadows in the room. Both brothers edged closer to Jax, but never breaking through the circle the candles made.

As the flames of the candles grew shadows appeared on the walls and as the shadows grew, they started to take shapes of things that weren't actually in the room. A scene started playing out in the shadows, one of two young women on the run through a forest, being chased by a very large wolf. The closer the wolf got to the girls the louder the growling got.

Almost as if in response to what was happening on the walls, as the wolf got closer Jax started thrashing around, still in whatever trance held him tight. His body started lifting into the air as his breathing evened out. A small blue light started edging out of his fingertips and toes. The wolf in the shadows turned to see a small ball of light form behind him, erasing any shadows it encountered. The two girls didn't appear to see it, still running for their lives, but the wolf saw it. The wolf turned and started running, not just towards to girls, but away from the light.

Jax started flexing his fingers, moving his hands around as if he was a puppeteer performing behind a curtain and controlling a puppet on stage. A slight breeze started to wrap around Jax, enough to start blowing out the flames of the candles around the room. The shadows started to disappear, but not before the wolf on the wall was tackled, for lack of a better word, by the ball of light, allowing the girls in the shadows to get away. The growling stopped the moment wolf and light collided. The rest of the candles blew out and Jax's body fell back to the table. Silence in the room, as Walker and Watson still stood on guard, not sure if that meant that everything was over.

Before they could think to much on it one last blast of wind swept through the room, accompanied by the haunted scream of half man/half beast who had been bested at his own game.

Suddenly Jax sat straight up while taking a deep breath in, his eyes popping open, and as his breath exhaled from his body he exclaimed,

"They're coming."

CHAPTER TWENTY-NINE

Haven

"Crawl if you have to!" Haven could see the satisfied smirk on James' face when he realized he was going to reach Nova before she could. He looked at Haven and winked, like the arrogant little shit that he was.

"You're mine, bitch." James was almost within arm's reach. The only reason he hadn't gotten to her yet was because of the crowd. That same crowd that was dragging Nova backwards was also starting to work against James and his men. They were also having trouble breaking through, though they were making more progress than Nova. The flow of the crowd wasn't making sense anymore. It wasn't natural, something was messing with people's minds, as they all seemed to be getting confused, turning around and walking back to where they came. When they would get back to the train they would stop, look around, and start walking back towards the exits. Not sure what was going on, the only thing that gave Haven hope was the slightly confused look on James' face when he realized he wasn't winning as easily as he was hoping to.

Haven started feeling something strange happening inside of her. Despite the confused crowd, the train was running on time, and she needed to be on it with Nova. She had never been this desperate, and for a moment she considered the possibility that she was having some type of heart attack or stroke. Her breathing was coming out rough, and it felt as if all of the nerves in her entire body were on fire. She was starting to get tunnel vision and she was fighting the urge to vomit.

But it was nothing physical that was causing these symptoms. What she didn't fully know in that moment was that her grandmother was right about her coming from a special blood line. Thousands of years may have separated her from her ancestors, but their blood still ran in her veins, singing with something special, and in that moment, when she really needed it, that connection to her ancestors was coming to help.

Unsure of quite what was happening, her hands started to tingle. Tingle and then slightly burn. She didn't want to let that distract her though, and she kept trying to reach for Nova. The crowd was finally starting to thin out, and the subway intercom let her know that the train would be pulling away any moment. She had to get on it and she had to make sure Nova was on it. It was their only hope. They could take it to the end of the line; there was a bus station just a few blocks from there, with no stops it would take them out of the city. But first she had to get to Nova.

"Haven!!!" Nova was screaming and crying, trying to push her way back to the one person that was there for her. Some people tried to get out of the way of this hysterical girl, others thought she was just being a brat and refused to move. Whatever confusion that the crowd had shared was starting to clear and Nova's hysterics were starting to get noticed. People were moving quickly out of the way, trying to ignore the dramatics going on.

Haven looked up from her hands and saw that James was within arm's length and about to grab the back of Nova's sweater. Haven threw her hands out as if to hold him off, but when she did something different happened.

It felt to her like a pulse came out of her hand, powerful enough that it knocked her on her ass and to knock any air out of her lungs. It took Haven a moment to realize she was staring at the ceiling. Slowly she sat up, her hand still humming, and as Haven looked up, she saw that, not only had she been knocked down, but so had everyone else on the platform. Knocked down and knocked out. Including James and his company. Everyone that is, except for Nova. The only person still standing, she looked just as confused and concerned as Haven.

"What the hell was that?" Her voice hoarse, Nova was standing there, shaking like a leaf, looking around at the ocean of bodies all around her, and then sending an accusing glance towards Haven.

"I ... I don't know ..." Haven scrambled to stand up, shaky and unsure of what just happened. It wasn't until the train started closing its doors for departure that she realized they had to get moving. The time for answers was not now, now was the time for running. James and his men were still knocked out, though it looked as if he was starting to come to.

"Come on!" Nova ran over to Haven, jumping over the unconscious crowd, grabbed her arm, and half dragger her onto the train. As the doors shut they looked back at a furious James, who was just sitting up. He looked around and saw the two girls on the departing train. In a furious rage he stood up and punched the closest pillar, dust and concrete was sent flying. Both girls breathed a sigh of relief once they could no longer see him. Haven threw an arm around Nova, giving her a side hug. Nova, needing more than that, threw her arms around Haven and held on tight.

Some-how they had gotten away. Somehow, they had thwarted James for a second time that night. There would be time to look for answers on what happened, but for now they just held on tight to each other, grateful that they were both still there.

The train ride was fairly quick, only a few stops before they were at the end. Still, they didn't waste any time getting off and finding the nearest bus depot. Haven took a moment to smooth down her clothes and run her hands through her hair before going into the bus station to buy the tickets with the wad of cash she had taken out earlier.

There was a bus leaving five minutes from when they bought the tickets and it felt like the longest five minutes of their lives. Neither girl really paid attention to their destination. Both were too busy scouring every shadow, worried that James would pop up out of nowhere. The speaker announced that their bus was boarding, and Nova had to stop herself from running to the bus. Trying to act casual Haven looped her arm through Nova's as they went to board the bus, comforting each other with their presence. The bus itself was fairly empty when they got on it and, without any further incident they were able to find seats near the back. The bus was empty enough that each girl took two seats to stretch out. Mere moments later the bus shut its doors and started pulling away from the depot. It wasn't until the bus depot was behind them that Nova allowed herself to get comfortable in her seat with a deep breath.

Neither girl said anything for a few minutes, letting the hum of the bus engine fill the silence. Trying to process what had just happened, now that the adrenaline was wearing off, Nova and Haven kept replaying everything in their own heads. Had it all happened the way they remembered?

Haven stared down at her hands, opening and closing them, looking for any sign that something abnormal had happened with them. All she could see were her normal hands. The tingling was completely gone, and the burning sensation was just a memory, but she was almost afraid to move her hands for fear of what could possibly happen.

Haven could feel Nova watching her from across the aisle with, what she assumed was confusion on her face. Haven would have been confused if she was Nova, too. Here Haven was, this random woman, who had put herself in danger just to help Nova out. In a world that appeared to be very selfish, Haven supposed someone helping in such a dire situation as this would come off as odd. Thinking on it, Haven had given up her job and her home, just to help Nova when no one else had believed her. If the situation was reversed, Haven would be overwhelmed with emotions, and she wouldn't know who to trust. Nova was the first to speak up, her voice was dry and cracked from screaming.

"Where are we going?" It was a simple question, Nova could have looked at her own ticket, but it was a sign to Haven that she was, in her own way, trying to reach out for comfort. Haven looked Nova up and down, really paying attention to what she was seeing. Nova was looking like the scared eighteen-year-old she was than in that moment. She was dirty, shaken up, and cowering in her seat. If Nova needed comfort, then Haven was more than happy to talk with her.

"Uh ..." Truth be told, Haven wasn't sure about that herself. Haven pulled out the bus tickets from her jacket pocket and started reading them.

"New Orleans apparently. Well ... that's going to be a long trip." They were at least half a day's ride to New Orleans, maybe even more if this bus started making stops at small towns along the way. Haven settled into her seat, attempting to at least appear as if she was relaxing, if only for Nova's benefit.

"Are your hands okay?" Nova croaked. Haven looked back down at them. Again, Haven had no idea. But Nova wasn't looking for anything but reassurance in that moment and that was something that Haven could give her.

"Yeah, they feel strange, but they're okay. We should get some sleep." Exhaustion was started to kick in, but Haven used it as a way to stop the questions. She needed a bit of time to think about a few things, and both of them needed to sleep. Haven and Nova snuggled into their respective chairs, getting as comfortable as they could while watching the nighttime scenery sail by. As she was drifting off Nova had one more thing to say.

"Haven?" She cleared her throat.

"Hmm?" Haven peeked an eye open to look at Nova, who had tears in her eyes, only this time they weren't tears of terror. They were of appreciation, and of hope.

"Thank you for not leaving me." Haven shared a look with Nova and a smile. As they made full eye contact with each other something inside of them clicked. A bond was formed, and Nova finally accepted that she was no longer alone in this. Haven thanked the heavens for that small step forward.

"You're very welcome." With that Haven closed her eyes, as did Nova, and they let the movement of the bus lull them into sleep.

CHAPTER THIRTY

Haven

The air smelled summer sweet, a combination of lilac bushes and that smell the air gets after a rainstorm hits a forest. That was the first thing that entered her mind. The second thing she noticed was that, instead of sleeping all crunched up on a bus seat, Haven seemed to be lying down on something soft and slightly damp with mildew.

Opening her eyes Haven winced slightly at the brightness of the sun. She slowly sat up and looked around at the field of tall grass and wildflowers that she was currently lying down in. The sun was impossibly bright, and yet, somehow, the sky above melted from light to impossibly dark and full of stars the farther up she looked. Haven's heart was beating itself almost right out of her chest. She had no memory of how she got here and, despite looking all around, there was no sign of Nova. Quickly standing up Haven tried keeping her breathing steady, fighting the urge to panic, knowing in the back of her mind it wouldn't do her any good. While Haven was unsure of what was going on, she could sense that she wasn't in any actual danger. The feeling of safety seemed to bloom in her chest the longer she thought about it and the longer she breathed in the sweet scents around her. It was as if the environment was weaving a spell upon her, lowering her defenses against her will.

"Nova ... Nova?" She started out whispering, hoping the girl was crouching behind a tree or lying down somewhere she just couldn't see. Haven started walking around, constantly whispering to her friend, just in case James was somehow responsible for the change in place. She could never be too careful. Unfortunately, there was still no sign of Nova, or anyone for that matter. At least not until Haven started walking down a trail leading out of the field and down to a small riverbed. As she got closer to the river Haven saw a hunched figure bent over, cleaning something with his hands in the water. Caught in a momentary paralysis caused by the surprise of finding a stranger in an otherwise abandoned area, Haven was torn. Whomever this was, he didn't look familiar. He wasn't one of the men that worked for James, at least not one that she had seen before, and to be honest he didn't look very threatening from where she stood. That being said, Haven had to decide if it was worth the risk. If she was wrong, she could be walking right into a trap. If she was right, maybe this stranger had some answers to the dozens of questions swarming her brain.

"I already know you're there, and if I wanted to kill you, you'd be dead by now." The man didn't look up from what he was doing, didn't move an inch, just kept cleaning an item in the river off, and item that she could see clearly.

"Time to stop playing shy and come on over." The voice was deep and rough. It had a calming lull to it, as if he was trying not to spook an anxious animal. Try as she might, Haven still wasn't able to move her body either way. She took a few deep breaths when the figure stood up fully and turned to her. His body seemed to tower over hers as she had to look up to see him fully. His face was young and pale; his grey eyes held warmth and friendliness. His hair was wild and dark, a nice contrast against his pale skin. His clothing choices were a little odd. It looked like he was wearing some type of cloak made of heavy fabric, possibly to keep the cold out of his bones, as the river held a chill in the air. The sleeves of his dark green tunic were pushed up, probably to keep them from getting wet while he messed around in the river. His pants were made of a dark brown material that looked more like they were made to be durable, not comfortable. To be blunt, he looked like he fell out of some fantasy book. As Haven took in his appearance he gave her a small smirk, letting her take a minute to work things out internally. Haven finally composed herself enough to start asking questions.

"Who are you?" Haven did her best to stare him down. The slight hostility in her voice seemed to go unnoticed as Jax casually stood there as if he was talking to an old friend.

"Jax." He pulled a set of leather looking gloves out of his back pocket and started to put them on his hands.

"Where are we?" Haven tried getting a closer look without actually moving. Something about his hands seemed off to her.

"That's not important." Each glove had a small button on the wrist that Jax took his time doing up. It was almost hypnotic, the way he moved deliberately but slowly, as if he had all the time in the world.

"Where's my friend?" Getting to the more urgent question Haven started getting more control over her body and she looked away from him, scanning the horizon for any sign of Nova, and still there was nothing. Jax looked at her in silence for a moment before answering.

"She didn't make the trip with you." Offering her no other information, Jax just stood there, watching her. It was clear that he was enjoying the back-and-forth banter, seemingly unconcerned about anything else. Haven, on the other hand, was starting to feel that panic bubbling back up at his response. Where was Nova?

"Yes, she did! We both got on that bus together!" Haven started towards him aggressively, pointing her finger at him as if it would force a better answer out of him. She was determined to find her friend, it was obvious, and Jax actually found it endearing. He threw his hands up in a defensive gesture.

"You misunderstand. Physically, you're still on the bus with her; it's your mind that's made this journey." What kind of new age bullshit was he trying to spout here? Haven gave him a skeptical stare before looking down at her own body, as if she just noticed her outfit was completely different from what she was wearing earlier. She stood there in a lavender and cream long sleeve dress. The sleeves had embroidered flowers on the cuffs. Her hair, no longer in her usual ponytail, was now half-up, half-down, with a few small braids dispersed in it. Just like something she would have seen in a fantasy movie, only this felt extremely real.

"Wait, what are you saying?" The momentary distraction of her own outfit was over and the words Jax was saying started echoing in her brain. Haven started noticing things, like the stillness all around them despite being on the edge of a forest. There were no birds chirping, no crickets or frogs croaking, it was silent in an almost eerie way now that she was focused on it. Jax lowered his hands.

"I'm saying, love, that you are something special. Someone special, and with that skill comes a vast array of perks that I'll have to fully explain to you some other time. You know, I thought I knew of all the protectors, a lot of them are gone now. I didn't think we were getting a new one at all anymore, but life keeps me on my toes, I guess, because here you are." Haven heard the words coming out of his mouth but none of them were making sense to her. Her brain started feeling fuzzy as she tried to glean anything real out of him. She wasn't anyone special, she was just Haven.

"I'm gonna ask this again, where are we? And what do you mean protectors?" Getting a straight answer out of this man may very well kill her, her patience already very short.

"The exact location is hard to place. It's a safe haven for people like us to meet up and help one another out. At least that's what I think it is, it's what I've used it for. I never really knew the official purpose of it, I just liked coming here." Jax turned from her and sat himself on a large rock just off to the side, still facing her.

"Okay, that's interesting, I guess. Look, I need to find my friend, it's kind of an emergency." Haven started pacing back and forth in front of him.

"I told you, she's right where you left her. When we're done here, you'll wake up on that stuffy bus." Jax looked at his wrist and, from seemingly out of nowhere, a modern-day watch appeared. Haven couldn't believe her eyes.

"Actually, we don't have much time left." Jax stood up and walked over to her, putting his hands on her shoulders.

"Time for what?" Haven tried backing away, but he wasn't letting go, not enough to hurt her but enough to let her know he was being serious.

"You're already headed my way. New Orleans, right?" There was that damn smirk again. Haven's head started to ache.

"How did you ..." Was he a danger, wasn't he a danger? The air started seeming slightly thinner, her breathes coming out shallow. Jax held a hand up to her mouth to silence her.

"We'll save more time if you just listen. I'm kind of off the grid but come to the Dusty Jacket and you'll find me. I'll answer all of your questions then."

"This is crazy." Haven started feeling dizzy, the ground was trying to come up to meet her, and she couldn't completely catch her breath, and the only thing really holding her up was Jax at this point.

"Yeah, you're gonna want to sit down. It gets easier the more time you spend in this place, but for now this isn't going to feel the best." Haven swayed and closed her eyes, trying to shake off her dizziness.

"Wha—"

Jax pulled his hands away.

"I'll see you soon." With that, everything went black. Haven fell to the ground, but before her body hit it she woke up, startled, on the seat of the bus, right beside Nova, who was looking at her with concern.

"Are you alright?" Haven sat straight up, looking around the entire bus, scanning for that familiar smirk. But he was no where to be found. Haven's heart was pounding, and she was sweating.

"What happened?" It took Haven a moment to remember everything that had just happened, or at least that she thought had happened. Nova had moved over from her own side of the aisle, trying to figure out what had made her friend wake up ready to swing at someone. Haven took a few deep breaths before looking at Nova.

"I'm not sure. I think you were having some type of nightmare, or a really intense dream." Nova helped Haven sit up properly and gave her a bottle of water. Was it all a dream? Haven could have sworn it was more than that. But it had been a big couple of days, her mind could have simply been working on overdrive.

"That was so strange ... and real." If she thought hard enough Haven could feel Jax's hands braced on her shoulders, holding her up. She could still smell the lavender and feel the slight wind on her face. Nova looked confused and concerned. The circles around her eyes showing Haven that she hadn't been sleeping while Haven had nodded off.

"What are you talking about?" If nothing else, Haven was grateful that Nova was sitting here, beside her. Whether or not it was real, Nova was real. She didn't need to be freaking Nova out just yet, especially if it was nothing but a figment of her imagination.

"Nothing, just a dream I guess." With that Haven leaned back into her chair and stared out at the changing landscape. Still, a small part of her couldn't let it go and she kept going over the entire conversation with the stranger by the river, over and over again, hoping some clue would show itself. After an hour of picking apart every piece of conversation with Jax, Haven was left with the memory of that smirk, and the dread that filled her with his statement, that she was someone special.

CHAPTER THIRTY-ONE

Haven

When the bus finally docked at the station, it was mid morning. The two girls made their way off the bus and away from any crowd. They had made it to New Orleans, and the feeling in the air was strange. With each breathe they took they felt a sense of calm, a sense of home. They knew they were in a city where the wacky and the weird were celebrated. They could only hope that it would become a place of sanctuary for them.

After her dream on the bus Haven was still weary of believing that the man from her vision was one that could help them. The issue was that they had no where else to go, no where to hide that didn't cost money, and if they kept spending Haven's money they would be on the streets within days. A warm breeze cooled the back of Havens' neck, went down her spine to her toes, and then back up to gently push her hair out of her face. It felt like the caress of, not a lover, but of a protector.

Nova watched Haven close her eyes and take a moment to herself. Nova was still somewhat lost in her own head. Numerous times on the bus Nova fell asleep only to find herself jumping awake with the fear that she was back in that room, back where she was completely helpless and by herself.

Haven opened her eyes, turned her head to the left, and as her eyes spotted a flyer taped to a light post Haven knew it was a sign. There, on the dirty light pole, surrounded by flyers for bands and local gigs, was one flyer, just one, for what looked like an eccentric bookstore called the Dusty Jacket. Haven knew in her gut that she needed to check it out, the flyer was there on purpose. With no other options Haven pointed it out to Nova.

"Well?" Nova asked.

"Maybe we should check it out?" Haven asked.

"If nothing else, it will get us off the street." Nova kept looking around, not feeling entirely safe despite all the miles between them and James. It would take awhile for Nova to feel comfortable in large crowds, and Haven could hardly blame her, what with everything she had been through.

"True. Let's go." Haven walked up to the flyer and tore it off the light post. Nova gave her a look.

"What? We need the address, and this way no one else will think this is where we went, that is if they are still following us." Nova just nodded her head as Haven took in the street signs and started walking in one direction.

They seemed to be making their way to the centre of the city, every street had something unique to look at and the eccentric people surrounding them kept Nova and Haven in a state of awe. The city had a heart, and it was beautiful.

While they were walking Haven had this nagging feeling in the back of her mind that she was supposed to be somewhere. It got to a boiling point and, after wandering for well over an hour, Haven could admit to herself that they were lost. Finally, she asked a few of the locals if there was a store or bar called the Dusty Jacket. She even showed them the flyer that she kept grasped in her hand. She received few blank looks at first, but finally she had found a lovely older lady that was able to point her in the right direction. Twenty minutes later she found herself standing in front of the most unique looking bookstore that she had ever seen.

The outside was painted a navy blue, but the paint looked worn in some places, as if the store had been there for decades. The glass door leading in stood by one of three giant display windows, giving Haven a glimpse into the store. It appeared, at least from the outside, to be void of customers, but books appeared to be piled from one end of the store to the other.

Nova took a glance at Haven.

"Well, shall we?" Haven nodded, and then grabbed Nova's arm for a moment.

"Promise me something. If this goes wrong, you get out. Find an exit, get out, and run." Panic flared in Nova's eyes, but Haven continued.

"I don't feel like this is a place we need to fear, but just in case, please, just please, get yourself out." Nova's eyes teared up at the thought of leaving Haven behind and running the other way, but she understood what Haven meant.

"Okay, I will. But that goes for you too." Nova barely squeaked it out, but Haven heard her and nodded in agreement. Not that she would actually just run out of Nova. She would do everything in her power to save Nova, but that wasn't the comfort Nova was looking for in this moment.

Haven reached over and took Nova's hand, and it wasn't until they stepped into the store that they noticed it wasn't only a bookstore, but there was a door on the far end of the room that appeared to lead to a bar.

Haven, while holding Nova's hand, kept Nova behind her, as an act of preservation. Looking around, Haven started taking it all in, the entire room of books that stood before them. It only took a moment before she noticed something odd about the books. None of the books were brand new. If anything, it looked like the place where all the lost, ripped, torn up books in the world ended up. The ones that were left on buses and under seats. It's as if they all ended up in this one store, placed on shelves, stacked in piles corner to corner. Nova also got lost to the strange ambience and didn't notice Jax until it was to late.

"I knew you would find me!" Haven and Nova jumped a mile, their hearts beating against their chests, and their clasped hand tightening on each other, before turning around. When they did, they saw, not five feet from them, a very real version of the guy from Haven's dream. Nova watched Haven's mouth drop open before Haven took her free hand and pointed it at Jax, shouting at him.

"You!" Haven was at a loss, she had almost convinced herself it was a dream, and not a vision, and yet here he stood. The only difference being his choice in clothing, which had a much more modern take than when he appeared in her head. Jax didn't seemed phased at all by the shock, anger, and confusion on both girls faces.

"Me! Hi, I'm Jax!" He turned and tried to introduce himself to Nova, who was getting more confused by the moment, by trying to shake her hand, but Haven stepped in between them, not letting him get close enough to do anything. Nova let go of Haven's hand and grabbed on to the back of her shirt, using Haven as a personal shield.

"No! Don't talk to her! You ... how ... what?" Haven wasn't trying to be quiet or polite anymore. She was full of questions, she was confused, and she wasn't about to let her guard down as Nova's protector. Jax threw his hands up in a defensive manner, as if to tell her with actions and not words that he was no threat to the two of them.

"Let me save you a few stuttered words there, love. I'm Jax, the guy you talked to in your dream." Both Haven and Nova scoffed at that, Haven taking that moment to assess Jax more clearly, looking him over from head to toe. As if he didn't see what she was doing, Jax continued on.

"Actually, it wasn't a dream. It was more like a vision, you were sort of astral projecting, but it's more complicated than that. We'll come back to that at a later time. But for now, I'm so glad to meet you two, safe and sound!"

The girls took a moment to look at each other, not quite believing this guy. He seemed friendly enough, and he wasn't giving off any concerning vibes. Maybe he was who he claimed to be.

"This must be the descendant of Little Red Riding Hood, it's a pleasure and an honor to meet you, my dear!" Jax kept trying to step around Haven, finally looking Nova in the eyes and still seeing the fear and exhaustion in them.

"From your rumpled appearance I take it that James Hunter is after you, right?" At the mention of his name both girls were back on guard, slowly backing away from Jax towards the exit. Strange as it may seem, when Haven turned and went to open the door to get out, it wasn't there. The door they had come in seemingly disappeared completely.

"What ... what ... just what? How do you know about him?" Nova couldn't get the fear out of her voice, no matter how hard she tried. Jax stopped trying to get closer and, instead, just focused on answering some questions.

"James and I go way back. But wait, just wait! It's not what you think. I can see you freaking out, but you misunderstand. I'm not working with James; in fact, I'm working against him. That's why you two are here, you just don't know it yet." Haven kept looking around for an exit, but constantly putting her body between Nova and Jax.

"Who the hell are you? Tell us right now or we walk!" She tried taking control of the situation, but Jax looked slightly uncomfortable talking about anything standing in the very public front area of his store.

"Can we go somewhere a bit more private? Perhaps the bar? You two look like you could use a good drink, set you right on your feet again." Was he trying to get them drunk so that they would lower their walls and be at his mercy?

"No, tell me right now!" Haven stood tall and spoke as confidently as she could. Jax nodded at her, as if conceding that he wasn't going to get his way just yet.

"Ok, demanding little thing, isn't she?" He looked at Nova's if they were conspiring together on the side.

"My name is Jax, and this is my store-slash-bar." He gestured around to the room they were in.

"Couldn't decide between the two?" Haven had zero patience, and apparently zero filter.

"No, just love them both the same, thank you. Now the reason you two are here is because you're being hunted, that's right hunted, by a guy named James Hunter." Every time Jax said his name Haven had to look around to make sure James wasn't coming around a corner. As if saying his name time and time again would some how summon him from whatever vile place he was currently residing in.

"How do you know all of this?" Haven started assessing Jax again, keeping an eye on that missing door.

"I've been waiting for you, Haven, waiting for you to find me. I was a little surprised when I saw you the first time, but it makes sense. If it's somewhere I can get to then of course you can get there too. You're the saviour after all." Everything Haven had been paying attention to fell to the side as Jax dropped that information in front of her.

"The what now?" She must have heard wrong. Or maybe it didn't mean the same thing to him.

"Savior." Jax said it so confidently that with almost no information about it or the situation, Haven almost believed him.

"Who's the saviour? Don't you dare say me, I'm not anyone's saviour!" Haven only wanted to make sure Nova was safe, but that didn't make her anyone's saviour. Jax took a moment before answering, looking over at Nova as he spoke softly.

"I know of one person who would disagree on that." Haven looked at Nova as well. Nova was looking back at Haven and Haven could see it in her eyes, the girl thought of her as a saviour.

"Look, there is no easy way to break you into this, especially if you're already being hunted down. It is you." Haven turned back to Jax.

"The saviour of what, exactly?" This guy kept talking in riddles and Haven wanted some real answers. Her patience was wearing thin. Unfortunately for her, all Jax gave her was more questions, and a very strange bedtime story.

"The saviour of our people. Look, this is all going to be hard to believe, but bear with me while I tell you a story, okay? It's the story of your ancestors, one that's supposed to be passed down from generation to generation. It should have been passed down to you, unless something went wrong. Anyway, as cliché as it sounds it starts off with once upon a time ..."

CHAPTER THIRTY-TWO

Jax

"Once upon a time, in an age long since forgotten, there was a small, peaceful village on the side of a mountain. The village itself was not easy to find, as it did not appear on any map found in the known world. If travelers happened to get close to the village a glamour would appear, making it look as if the village was nothing but a large patch of trees. Any unwanted or unexpected person would feel the need to keep walking, a sense of danger tickling the bottom of their spine the longer they lingered there.

"It wasn't as if the people living in the village were bad people, they were very much the opposite. They were a group of the most kind, most honourable, and simply the sweetest townsfolk. The effort they put in to keep people away from their village had nothing to do with wanting to keep their resources to themselves. Instead, it was about keeping their secret safe from the rest of the world.

"Most, if not all of the townsfolk, found themselves to be from extra-ordinary families. Families who, generation after generation, experienced talents- or gifts- that made their lives easier and a bit more majestic. Every family would specialize in a different form of magic that they would then use to help their village flourish. The village elders knew that if any outsiders heard about their skills the village would find itself flooded with requests and demands, some more sinister than others. In an effort to keep their families safe it was decided generations ago to put up the glamour, and the village had been living in peace ever since.

"Now the village itself was self-sustaining, either by growing everything they needed on the mountain, or using their abilities to gather whatever they may have been missing. Therefore, it's citizens never thought much about wandering to different towns or even off of the mountain. And because of the glamour, they hadn't seen any strangers turn up in decades.

"That is, until two travelers stumbled into this small village one morning, just after the sun had risen over the mountain top. The village people all froze, unsure of what to do about it. No one spoke to them, mothers started ushering their young children indoors, and the reception itself was icy, to say the least.

"The two travelers, Jacob and Wilhelm, were brothers, and while not oblivious to the odd reception, they continued on into town. They were storytellers and they travelled the world to pick up stories that they could write down and share with others. When they found this town, they knew that they had found something special, so they decided to stay for awhile. The town towns people were a little apprehensive around them, but eventually they became one of the locals, and the locals shared their secrets with the brothers, the secrets of magic. They even tried teaching the brothers a bit of magic, but the brothers were adamant, all they wanted to take with them were the stories. They promised to change everyone's names for safety, but they wanted to tell of the adventures of this small town. With good-versus-evil, creatures in the night, and good surviving everything, the brothers struck a gold mine. True to their word the only thing that they took with them when they left town were the stories. What they didn't know was that the parchment they purchased to write everything down on had special properties and a better memory than most people. For those pages bound these two brothers to that village forever.

"When they were leaving the town, they had to swear not to tell anyone where the town was in order to keep its occupants safe. For while it was a charming town the people that lived there were not without faults, and some of them even had enemies that were looking to destroy them. As the two brothers were leaving, they had to swear an oath. This oath bound them to the protection of the town. That one oath is why now, hundreds of years later you're being called upon. See, Haven, when they spoke the words of the oath they were standing on sacred ground, and that oath will be attached to their blood line until the end of days."

CHAPTER THIRTY-THREE

James

Damn it! He had them! Both of them! They were trapped, they were within his grasp, how did they get away! He was surrounded by fools! James fisted his hair in both hands, trying to calm the storm brewing inside of him. He pressed the button on his earpiece, and his entire team was listening, waiting for instruction.

"Haven's apartment. Everyone. Now." With that he turned his earpiece off and ran to meet up with his team. They had a lot of ground to make up and someone better have some answers for him, or he was going to start snapping necks.

By the time James got to Haven's apartment his entire team was already there, the only thing stopping him from "firing" any of them. They had already begun tearing apart Haven's apartment, under the guise of investigating a gas leak. James hoped to find clues as to where those girls were headed. Now that her grandmother was dead there was nothing keeping either of them in the city. He had already sent a team to each bus station, train station, and airport in the vicinity. These were two helpless girls working alone while he had a full team at his disposal. James hoped that if he threw enough manpower at the situation they would be caught quickly. He no longer cared how bad it looked to the board, he no longer cared about keeping this a quick and quiet job.

Watching his team was almost painful at this point. They were being methodical and careful, but the time for that had past. James started throwing her bookcases to the ground, making sure to leave no stone unturned. James frantically searched her drawers, throwing her clothes across the room, still not finding anything. He started getting more and more upset as his search turned up nothing. It was only a matter of time before someone called the cops, if they hadn't already, with the noise he was making smashing Haven's dishes against the wall and slashing at her mattress. A feral growl ripped out of his throat while his team slowly started backing up against the door, careful to stay out of his way and avoiding eye contact.

The entire apartment was trashed, and yet they didn't find one single clue as to where Haven took Nova. James looked around at the carnage while trying to calm his breathing. It was time to send a message to this girl who dared get involved in his business. If he couldn't do it physically, he would have to settle for doing it symbolically. Piling her books in the middle of the living room James snapped his fingers and one member of his team handed him a gas can. James took great pleasure pouring it over top of Haven's books. His team slowly started making their way out of the apartment and into the unmarked cars in the parking lot.

Once her books were thoroughly coated James made sure to splash some on the curtains, on her bed, even on her pantry doors. Without so much as a second thought, without looking to make sure his team was out and safe, James pulled out a lighter from the left pocket of his jacket, rolled it across his leg to light it, tossed it onto the pile of books, and walked out of the apartment.

The parking lot was empty of his people by the time he walked out of the building, and that's when he heard the fire alarms starting to go off. Almost instantly the other residents of the building were coming down the stairs and gathering in the parking lot for safety.

Without looking back to see the carnage that he created, James just quietly slipped into the night like a shadow intent on revenge.

CHAPTER THIRTY-FOUR

Haven

Haven wanted to roll her eyes at what Jax was saying. She wanted to throw sarcasm at him, turn and walk out the door. The story itself was almost too easy, a bit stereotypical even. She somehow was related to two of the best fairy tale writers known in the modern world, and because of that very unlikely fact, she had an obligation to protect a bunch of strangers. It sounded like gold threaded bullshit, if she were being honest. The only thing that kept her from running in the opposite direction, other than trying to keep Nova safe, was a small spark in her gut. The type of feeling that had her wondering "what if". The odds that Jax was telling the truth were so small— but what if? What if everything he was saying was right, and it was her destiny, her fate to stand between evil and the people of this town?

"Great story. But what does that have to do with me?" Jax could see the hesitancy on Haven's face, and the doubt that clouded Nova's eyes. He stayed true to the story, though, and kept talking, hoping something that he said would make an impact.

"The two brothers, Jacob and Wilhelm, were the Grimm Brothers, and they were your great, great, great, great uncles. Their blood runs through your veins, you are being called upon to help those in need. That includes their descendants. Which is where young Nova here comes in."

In that moment Haven realized that, in all reality, if it were right, that would mean that Nova was a descendant of someone in that town. Fairy tale characters aside, the odds that Nova's ancestors and her ancestors had once met on a different continent, Haven's brain was aching from all the mental leaps she was putting it through.

"Me? What do I have to do with any of this?" Nova had a deer in the headlights look about her, but who could blame her at this point if the story was going right over her head. Haven was surprised Nova was still standing and not rocking back and forth in a corner somewhere. Jax looked at Nova and gave her a caring smile.

"Haven't you wondered why this guy is hunting you down?" Jax managed to ask the question in a way that didn't imply Nova was stupid, but instead had her perking up to listen.

"I just assumed it was some type of stalker-slash-murderer thing. That or for money, isn't that why most people commit crimes these days?" It was an answer created to take any attention off of Nova specifically. Haven could see that Nova was looking for reasons to blend in, because if there was nothing distinct about her then maybe one day this would all blow over and she could go back to her old life. However, Haven knew it would take more than wishful thinking to stop James.

"Nova, look, I don't want to scare you any more than you've been scared. But I do want to make sure you understand fully the situation that you're in. What James is doing isn't random. Everything he has done up to this point, and everything he's going to do in the future, has a reason behind it, a purpose. See, James has ancestors too. And his ancestors had a big vendetta against yours for reasons that may have gotten lost over time, but as long as your relatives stayed in that town the magic protected them. They could not be found. Really, it has only been in the last hundred years that occupants of that town started moving across the globe. They've managed to do it under the radar, until now. Something had to have happened, but James is out for blood, for his family. They've had these stories making their way through generations as well, and now James is trying to finish off what his predecessors started hundreds of years ago. They are trying to kill off every family that lived in that small town." The breath got knocked out of Haven a bit. A town full of people in hiding, there had to be more to the story. This just kept getting bigger and bigger. It was only yesterday where it was Haven and Nova against James. Now it was multi-generational, not to mention magic existed and somehow was a major factor.

"That's horrible! Why hasn't anyone brought this to the police?" Not that Haven thought the police would do anything. If the officer that came to her after she was attacked was anything to go on, the police were useless in this situation. James and his family held power and there wasn't anything Haven could do to change that.

"They can't. For one, James has family in the justice system all over the country, so he's pretty much untouchable legally. For another, they have magic on their side. The magic from that mountain has followed the descendants throughout the decades, but because they stopped using it for fear that it would lead their enemy's right to them the magic is dormant. No one is trained for it anymore. However, James' family has kept up the practices and anything the law can't do for them magic can."

They were still listening to him, which was a bit surprising. Jax would stand there all day and answer their questions if it meant that they were starting to believe.

"This sounds crazy, you know that right? Magic towns, fairy tales, vendettas and blood oaths spanning hundreds of years ... what makes you think any of this is more than just a fancy story?" Grasping at anything she could, Haven was trying to make was Jax was saying make sense.

"Because my family has been a part of it too." Talk about dropping a bomb. The room was quiet for a moment as both Nova and Haven absorbed that piece of information. Nova was the first to break the silence.

"Where do they fit in?" Her voice was the quietest out of the three, but the silence in the room allowed for her to be heard. Without waiting a beat, without batting an eyelash, Jax look directly at Nova and answered.

"We are the message." A sense of dread filled Haven and she couldn't stay silent anymore.

"The message?" This was getting ridiculous, but to his credit Jax didn't let the disbelief in Haven's voice deter him or turn him sour. He simply looked at Haven and kept talking.

"It has been our job for many years to keep the stories alive. We are here in case the need to protect these people arises. If that need does, then we help the saviour, which would be you, find the lost souls and gather them together so that they can be protected." Haven's head started to spin again, and it felt like the oxygen in the room was getting sparse. For the most part she was open minded, but this was all just piling together in a lump of madness.

"This is crazy, this is to much! She isn't Little Red Riding Hood!" Haven gestured towards Nova, who looked like she was having her own issues with the information dump going on. Jax stepped up, again, and asked a question that rendered both girls speechless.

"Really? Then why is she being chased by the wolf?" Nova's jaw dropped and Haven's eyes almost bulged out of her head. She was almost certain she hadn't mentioned anything about a wolf, or the dreams that she had shared with Nova to Jax. Was it just a lucky guess, or was there some truth to his crazy story? Whatever it was, Haven was no longer leaving the building. At least not until she got some clear answers out of him.

"Ladies, listen, I could stand here all day and have this conversation with you. But I need you to know that this is more than a debate about fictional characters. In order for you to have any hope in defeating James, you need to believe. Now, I don't expect you to listen to me without presenting you with proof. I know this is a lot, and it sounds absolutely batty, but let me introduce you to a few people. Just listen to their story, and if you still don't believe me then you can walk out of here and I won't bother you again." Haven and Nova looked at each other, as if they were having a silent conversation. A few eye movements and hand gestures later they both turned to Jax and nodded their heads.

Jax led out of the room, down a hallway, and into what appeared to be an Irish bar, or pub. It was mostly empty, except for one guy behind the bar and one guy sitting on a stool. From the briefest glance it was obvious that they were twins. They were having a lively debate and didn't see Jax lead the girls into the room.

"I'm telling you, that whole dream thing he does is going to freak her out, there is no way that they are going to show up here." Guy Number One was behind the bar, wiping down empty pint glasses with an off-white towel. His brother sat on a stool in front of the bar with a half empty pint in front of him and a bowl of pretzels that he was casually munching on.

"Have a little faith man, you never know. People can surprise you. I mean, we believed him and here we are." Guy number two gestured to the room without actually looking around it.

"Willing to put your money where your mouth is on that one?"

"You think I won't??" The man sitting down stood up, pushing his stool over but the one behind the bar kept his casual stance. Jax shook his head silently before getting their attention.

"Gentlemen!" Both guys looked up from their intense debate and saw three pairs of eyes staring at them. The guy in front of the bar broke out into a goofy smile as he pointed to the girls behind Jax.

"I told you man, dudes got some Jedi mind shit worked out." The man behind the bar put down his pint glass and came out from behind the bar to greet them. Jax just shook his head and led the girls further into the pub. Nova stayed just behind Haven, and to the side a bit, using Haven as a bit of a shield from the strangers.

"Ignore them, they're still getting use to this whole thing. Please come in, have a seat. We'll get you a drink." Jax gestured to the bar as Watson picked up his stool from the ground. The girls joined him at the bar, ensuring that no one was between them and the door. Haven couldn't help but be paranoid, not with everything that they had already been through. Watson went back behind the bar and started serving up soda to everyone as a way of breaking the ice.

Once everyone had a drink there was an awkward silence as everyone tried to measure everyone else up in their own minds. The twins kept looking between Jax and the girls, Haven kept her eyes on Jax and the door, Nova kept her eyes on the bar, not wanting to draw any attention at all, and Jax took his time observing the entire room. A few moments in Haven couldn't take it anymore. They were wasting valuable time.

"I don't want to rush you with this story, but we're only giving you ten more minutes before we high tail it outta here."

Nova tensed, as if preparing her body for the inevitable fight when they tried walking out of there on their own. Jax clapped his hands.

"Right. So, ladies, this here is Walker and Watson. They're brothers that found me a few weeks ago, or I guess I found them and then they found me. Guys, this is Haven, the one I was telling you about, and her charge Nova."

Nova finally looked up from the bar, making eye contact with Walker first, and then Watson. Haven watched her closely, ready to jump in any time she was needed. Instead, Haven saw Nova's shoulder relax and a small smile grace her lips. She didn't appear to be panicking at all. Who were these men, and why did it seem like Nova was completely comfortable around them? Walker directed a question at Nova and Haven was proud of the way she didn't hesitate to answer him.

"Nova? Interesting name." Nova nodded.

"Yeah, apparently I'm Little Red Riding Hood's descendent. Who are you two suppose to be related to?" A small bond had formed in that room, one that needed to be nurtured and grow, but the start of it was there. Haven decided that if Nova could find something in common with these two then they should stick around. Maybe then Nova would no longer feel so alone.

"It's kind of a long story-" Watson piped up, not sure where Haven and Nova were at believability wise.

"When isn't it? Start talking boys." Haven was doing her best to keep it all together, but if she had to sit here while everyone made small talk for another second she was going to explode.

"Straight to the point, alright. Well, it all started I guess when my brother Watson and I were getting ready for our annual road trip. Every year we like to jump in the car and just drive for a few days, see what kind of adventure we can get ourselves into ..." The women settled in as Walker and Watson took turns telling their tale. A tale that sounded familiar, a tale of just how dangerous strangers could be, a tale of an adventure that a pair of siblings went on while walking through the woods...

To Be Continued in Book 2

Gratitude

Thank you to all those who have believed in me, even during the moments I didn't believe in myself. To my friends and family, the support you all have shown me over the years has been beautiful. I appreciate you.

I want to thank Charlie Biddiscombe from Eyesight Publishing for creating the cover of this book, it's beautiful!

I want to thank Katie for being my developmental editor. The way you built up my confidence as a writer, and yet were able to give me notes that bettered the story in so many ways, is something I'll never forget.

I want to thank my ARC readers for volunteering to read an unpublished novel from an unknown author.

To anyone who picks this book up to read, thank you. Thank you for being here at the start of my journey.

About the Author

Chelsea was born in Edmonton, Alberta and got her Bachelor of Arts degree from the University of Calgary. She resides in a small town outside of Edmonton with her partner and their three children. Chelsea has always been an avid reader and dreamed of one day having her very own novel gracing the shelves of the local libraries and bookstores.

Awakening Fate is Chelsea's debut novel, book one in the Intertwined trilogy.

www.ingramcontent.com/pod-product-compliance
Lightning Source LLC
Chambersburg PA
CBHW020115180626
46812CB00006B/2613